MORGAN'S WAR

Owen Morgan, fearless mercenary, had not come back to his childhood island home to recapture the hope and joyful memories of his youth—he had come to kill. But he would soon learn how dangerous it was to go home again.

The girl he loved was now warming the bed of a Nazi. The man he had virtually worshipped was a cheerful host to the enemy. The American Ranger, Morgan's second-in-command, turned Morgan's stomach with his sadistic violence. Ironically, a German soldier turned out to be the only man on the island whom he admired.

And worst of all, the Nazi commander who was his quarry now held him captive—and had set a date for his execution.

Morgan's war seemed almost over.
It was not.
It had just begun . . .

A GAME
FOR HEROES

James Graham

A DELL BOOK

Published by
DELL PUBLISHING CO., INC.
1 Dag Hammarskjold Plaza
New York, N.Y. 10017

Dell ® TM 681510, Dell Publishing Co., Inc.

ISBN: 0-440-13262-2

Reprinted by arrangement with
Doubleday & Company, Inc.

Printed in the United States of America
Previous Dell Edition #3262

New Dell Edition
First printing—July 1978

For my wife and children
who know Steiner's beach well ...

Men generally die in war when they cannot help it and are defeated by a disadvantageous situation.

Wu Ch 'i.

AUTHOR'S NOTE

The German occupation of the Channel Islands from 1940-45 is a matter of history, but the island of St Pierre exists on no map of the area to my certain knowledge, which hardly makes it necessary for me to add that all characters and incidents in this present story are fictional. No reference is made, or intended, to any living person.

J. G.

Contents

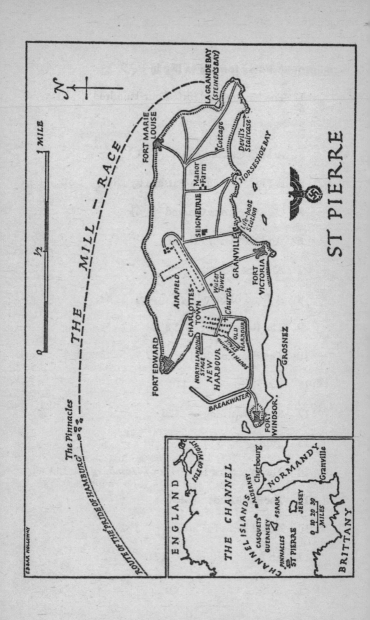

PROLOGUE A Fine Morning to Die in

The bodies started to come in with the tide just after dawn, clustered together, bobbing in through the surf to the beach a hundred feet below my hiding place.

The bay was called Horseshoe for obvious reasons. As a boy, I had swum down there on more occasions than I could remember and there was an excellent beach when the tide was out. An inhospitable shore now though, seeded with mines and choked by barbed wire strung between rusting steel lances. No place to be, alive or dead, on a cold April morning.

It was raining slightly and visibility was not good in the dawn mist so that even Fort Victoria on its rocky point a quarter of a mile away was barely visible.

I took a cigarette from my waterproof tin, lit it and sat there watching more bodies float in, but not from any morbid curiosity. It was impossible for me to leave the shelter of those gorse bushes before nightfall. If I attempted to move in daylight, capture was certain on such a small island, especially now that my presence was known.

Five years of war had left me indifferent where death was concerned, even to its uglier aspects. The time when a body had any emotional effect was long since gone. I had seen too many of them. The fact of death was all that mattered. Down there, British and German floated together and at that distance, it was impossible to distinguish between them, which proved something.

Another wave slopped in, flinging a body high in the air, casting it farther up the beach than the others. As it landed, a mine exploded, tossing it up again, arms flailing wildly as if there was still life there. What was left was flung across the wire to hang like raw meat.

It was perhaps ten minutes later that the next one floated in, supported by a yellow life-jacket. The sea retreated with a great sucking noise, leaving the body face down. It seemed to move slightly. At first I thought I was mistaken. A trick of the light or the fact that even in shallow water, it behaved differently from the others because of the inflated life-jacket.

But I was wrong, for as the curtain of green foam slopped in again, an arm was raised to claw at air and I seemed to hear a faint cry as the man was pushed towards the wire.

For the next two or three minutes, succeeding waves failed to reach him. He lay there as if exhausted, then tried to push himself up as a great comber rolled in and flattened him. When it receded, he was still alive, but there could only be one end to the game that was being played down there.

I crouched in the shelter of the gorse bushes, waiting for something to happen. Anything that would make it unnecessary for me to play at heroes. It came from an unexpected quarter, the fold in the cliffs on my right from which a narrow track dropped to the beach.

I heard voices first, calling excitedly, then half-a-dozen men appeared and paused on the brow of the hill about fifty feet above the sea. They were Todt workers, a few of the poor wretches brought over from France to labour on the island's fortifications. This lot were a road gang from the looks of them and carried picks and shovels. There were no guards, which wasn't unusual. The island, after all, was as effective a prison in itself as could have been found anywhere.

They seemed to be having an argument, then one of them moved ahead and started to slide down the slope to the beach below. He dropped the last ten or fifteen feet into soft sand, picked himself up and approached the wire. He was a brave man, and closer to death than he perhaps knew.

Another great wave rolled in, washing a second body into the minefield. There was a sudden eruption and for a moment, the sea boiled. When it drew back, I was surprised to see that the man in the yellow life-jacket was still alive.

But not for much longer. He needed a miracle now and from the looks of it, it would have to be a miracle called Owen Morgan. I realised that with a kind of weary fatality as the Todt worker on the beach, who had thrown himself flat on his face, got up and paused uncertainly. He knew about the mines now and only a fool would venture into such a death trap—a fool or someone who didn't particularly care whether he lived or died.

I took the Mauser with the S.S. bulbous silencer from

the clip at the rear of my belt and slipped it into the pocket of my reefer coat. Then I took the coat off and pushed it into the crevasse at the back of the overhang under which I was sheltering. I transferred my knife to my right-hand pocket. The spring blade action meant that I could open it with one hand which might be useful down there in the water.

What else was there? My identity discs. I checked that they were safe in the secret pocket in my belt, not that they were likely to do me much good where I was going. And the black patch which covered what was left of my right eye—I almost forgot about that. It was hardly likely to remain in place in the kind of surf that was coming in and I pulled it down around my neck on its elasticated band.

In the country of the blind, the one-eyed man is king. God knows why I thought of that as I went down a narrow crevasse for twenty or thirty feet and emerged on to a shoulder of rock. The Todt workers on the hillside saw me at once, but the man on the beach was back at the wire looking for a way through.

'No good—too many mines,' I shouted in French. 'Leave it to me.'

He turned and looked up in surprise, staring dumbly, so I gave it to him in English and German for good measure. Some little way below, a rock jutted out thirty feet or so above deep water. When I was twelve, I had jumped from it to impress Simone. She had refused to speak to me for a week for the fright I had given her. It all came back so clearly as I paused there for a moment.

A good morning—a fine morning to die in. I took a quick breath and jumped.

It was cold—cold as only the Channel can be with the Atlantic rolling in all the way from Newfoundland. I went deep and kicked with all my strength as the current caught me.

I was wearing canvas rope-soled shoes, denim pants and a Guernsey fisherman's sweater and all these things I had retained by design. If you are swimming in cold waters, clothes help to retain body heat and so it was now. I surfaced and started to swim the hundred yards that separated me from Horseshoe.

The great tidal surge that drives in through the Channel Islands, raises the level of the water in the Golfe de

St. Malo by as much as thirty feet and I could feel the
implacable force of it pushing me forwards, lifting the
waves into whitecaps in a great unbroken progression to
crash in across the beach.

The swimming in itself was no great feat. All I had to
do was stay afloat and the tidal current did the rest. I was
aware of the Todt workers up on the hillside in the green
fold between the cliffs, of the man on the other side of the
wire and then a great wave took me in its iron grip and
carried me in at what seemed like a considerable speed.

I touched sand, reached out for some sort of secure anchorage and found myself high on the beach as the sea
drained away. The man in the yellow life-jacket was no
more than ten yards to my left. Another wave washed in
as I got to one knee. As it receded, I was already on my
feet and moving to join him.

He was perhaps seventeen, a young German naval rat-
ing, a telegraphist according to the badge on his sleeve.
His left shoulder and arm were a bloody mess which certainly explained his inability to help himself.

He was actually reaching out for the wire as I got to
him and I dropped to one knee and turned him over. His
eyes were dark glass, staring through and beyond me, no
comprehension there at all and he was obviously in deep
shock. I got an arm around him as another wave washed
over us. When I shook the salt water from my eyes and
looked across the wire, the Todt workers were moving
down the path in company with three German soldiers,
two of whom carried machine pistols.

One of them called to me, but his voice was drowned
by the roaring of another incoming wave. And then, in
the silence that followed, a horse whinnied and I looked
up and saw Steiner sitting on a grey mare on the brow of
the hill.

He called to the men below, telling them to stay where
they were and they obeyed instantly which didn't surprise
me for he was that kind of man. He went down the path
to join them, there was a quick conversation and then one
of the soldiers scrambled back up the path to where the
mare grazed peacefully and disappeared over the brow of
the hill.

The other two herded the Todt workers back and
Steiner came down on his own carrying three stick gre-

nades in his left hand. He wore a three-quarter length
coat with a black fur collar which I happened to know
was standard issue to Russian officers of staff rank only
and his Brandenberger forage cap was tilted at the exact
regulation angle and no more.

He smiled as he stopped on the other side of the wire. 'I
had expected you long gone by now, Owen Morgan. What
happened?'

'The best laid schemes and all that.' I said. 'Does it
matter?'

'Not really. What have you got there?'

'One of yours—a telegraphist from the E-Boat.'

'Will he live?'

'I should imagine so.'

'Good. Stay exactly where you are.'

He moved twenty or thirty yards away along the beach
and another wave crashed in. It was a big one—large
enough to have us both across the wire and I hung on
grimly with everything I had.

The boy was unconscious, I was aware of that as I surfaced and at the same time saw Steiner toss the first grenade over the wire. There was a double explosion, followed by a third as mines started to detonate each other.
He had turned his back briefly and I lost sight of him
through a curtain of smoke and sand. As it cleared, he
moved in closer, examined the ragged gap in the beach
defences he had created, then tossed the second grenade.

The waves washed in again, stronger than ever and I
was beginning to tire. It had been a long night and this
was a hell of a morning to follow. As I came up for air,
the third grenade landed. There were four quite distinct
explosions and, as the echoes died away, sand and smoke
lifted in a dense cloud.

Birds called, wheeling high above, rising from the cliff
face, razorbills, shags, gulls and a lone storm petrel came
in low through the smoke like a bomber on its final run,
straight and true, skimming the waves as it turned out to
sea.

Steiner was standing at one end of the ragged path he
had blasted through the wire to the water's edge. He
waved and I called out to him sharply.

'Careful—no guarantee you've got them all.'

'Only one way of finding out.'

He walked through as calmly as if he were taking a

Sunday afternoon stroll in the park, pausing only to kick a ragged nest of wire out of the way and splashed towards me.

There was a sudden roar of an engine as a VW field car appeared and braked on the brow of the hill. Several soldiers got out and started down towards the beach. Steiner ignored them.

'I'm sorry about this, but there is little I can do now, you understand that?'

'Naturally.'

'Have you any weapons?'

'My knife only.'

'Give it to me.'

He slipped it into his pocket and got a hand under the young sailor's arm. 'Let's get him out of here before he dies on us. This business might help you considerably.'

'With a man like Radl? You must be joking.'

He shrugged. 'All things are possible . . .'

'In this worst of all possible worlds.' I misquoted. 'You look after Simone, that's all I ask, and forget that last night ever happened. Just keep her out of this. Don't waste your time on me. I'm a dead man walking, we both know that.'

'You sacrificed yourself to save a German seaman. That must count for something. Even Radl has been known to listen to reason on occasion.'

'From a sergeant-major?' I laughed. 'Not a habit of many colonels that I've known in most armies, including my own. He'll show you the door and more than that.'

'Oh, no,' he said softly. 'Never that, my friend,' and he was no longer smiling.

We ploughed through the surf, the boy between us, and stumbled through the gap. The men who waited on the other side were military police, as conspicuous in their brass breatsplates as British army redcaps. There were four of them, three corporals and a major. Two of them took the boy from us, laid him down carefully on a stretcher and gave him some quick first-aid.

Steiner had walked a yard or two away, brushing sand from his coat. The major came forward and looked me over. 'Who are you?' he demanded in bad French.

I suppose he didn't know what to make of me which was hardly surprising considering the clothes I was wearing and the jagged scar that cut across the empty socket where my right eye had been and bisected the cheek, didn't help much. I adjusted the eye patch.

Steiner answered for me. 'Major Brandt,' he said, 'this gentleman is a British officer who has just sacrificed his freedom to save the life of a German sailor.'

And Brandt took it without a murmur, including the tone of voice. He hesitated fractionally, then turned to me and said in quite reasonable English. 'You will please identify yourself.'

'My name is Morgan. My service number is 21038930. My rank is Lieutenant-Colonel.'

He clicked his heels and produced a silver cigarette case. 'May I offer you a cigarette, Colonel? You look as if you could do with one.'

I took it and the light which followed and drew the smoke into my lungs with conscious pleasure. It might, after all, be close to my last.

'And now,' he said politely, 'I must ask you to accompany me to the Platzkommandantur in Charlottestown where Colonel Radl, the acting governor of St Pierre, will no doubt wish to speak with you.'

A nice way of putting it. I started forward and Steiner got in the way. He had the Russian field coat off and was holding it ready for me. 'With the colonel's permission,' he said, a slight, ironic smile on his mouth.

It was only when I pulled it on and felt the warmth of the fur lining that I realized how cold I was. 'Thank you, Sergeant-Major,' I said. 'For this among other things.'

His heels clicked together and the salute he gave me would have warmed the heart of the most demanding drill instructor the Brigade of Guards could have supplied.

I turned and followed the stretcher up the hill.

The drive into Charlottestown was the strangest experience of all so far. There were the cobbled streets, the houses that were a mixture of French Provincial and English Georgian, the gardens high-walled against the constant winds. Everything was the same as it had always been and yet not the same.

It wasn't the concrete pill boxes, the barbed wire, the bomb damage down at the harbour, the more obvious signs of war. It was the signposts in German as well as English, the incongruity of seeing an S.S man pausing to light a cigarette outside the old post office with a sign on the wall that still read *Royal Mail* and the sight of grey-green uniforms and cars with swastikas painted on them parked in a square with a name like Palmerston. It all combined to give a curious air of unreality to things, that I found difficult to shake off.

The field car dropped us in the square and departed with the injured sailor and we walked the rest of the way, climbing the steep cobbles of Charlotte Street, past shops that stood empty now. Windows were broken everywhere, paint peeling, and there was a general air of decay. Not surprising after five years of occupation.

The Platzkommandantur, headquarters of the German civilian administration, although there were few enough of them to administer on St Pierre, was housed in what had been the island branch of the Westminster Bank before the war. I'd had an account there, still had by all the rules, which made it an interesting experience to go in through the arched granite porch to the cool interior.

Three uniformed clerks worked industriously on the other side of the mahogany counter and the two sentries on either side of the door to what had once been the manager's office were S.S. paratroopers and as hard-bitten a looking pair as I'd seen in many a long day with an Iron Cross second class apiece and the ribbon for the Campaign against Russia. They'd come a long way from Stalingrad or wherever it had been.

Brandt went in first and we waited. Steiner made no attempt to speak and stood at the window looking out into the street. Within a couple of minutes, Brandt called for him and he went in. I waited and the two S.S. men stared beyond me into space and then the door opened and Brandt reappeared.

'Please to come in, Colonel Morgan,' he said in English, and as I went forward he called the two guards to attention.

I think it was Radl's physical presence that was the most astonishing thing about him. The sheer bloody size of the man. He must have been six foot three or four at least and couldn't have weighed less than sixteen or seventeen stone.

My impression was that he had been working in his shirt sleeves for he was still buttoning his tunic as I entered. I noticed several things in that first swift glance.

The S.S. insignia on his collar and the medals, which included the Deutsches Kreuz worn on the right side in gold which meant it had been awarded for courage in the face of the enemy, and the Gold Party Badge which was only awarded to those who had been members of the Nazi Party before its accession to power in 1933.

And his face with the great jutting brow and deep-set eyes, was the face of some fanatical Roundhead, the kind of man who could cry on the Lord with fervour, pray out loud on his knees and in the same breath, cheerfully interpret the master's word as burning young women alive for witches.

He stayed in his seat, both hands on the desk. 'Your name, rank and number.'

His English was poor and I replied in German. He showed not the slightest surprise and continued in the same language. 'You can prove this?'

I fiddled about on the inside of my belt and produced my identity discs. I passed them across and waited as he examined them gravely. He put them down and snapped a finger at Brandt, not Steiner.

'A chair for the colonel.'

I shook my head. 'I'll stand. Let's get it over with.'

He didn't attempt to argue, but got to his feet, I suppose because it offended his sense of what was fitting that two senior officers should not be on terms of perfect equality, even if he did intend to have me shot that same afternoon.

He sat on the edge of the desk. 'Owen Morgan? Now that I find interesting. Did you know that the lifeboat on this island bears that name?'

There seemed no reason to hide the fact. 'After my father, I was born and raised here.'

'So?' He nodded. 'That explains a great deal. You were here to find out what you could about the Nigger project.'

It was a statement of fact, well-timed and delivered in a perfectly normal conversational tone as he took a cigarette from a sandalwood box and lit it.

I didn't bite. 'Was I?'

'Four of your companions are alive and in our hands. Two more were recovered from the harbour. One of them spoke a little before he died and what he said was informative.'

'I'm sure it was.'

He carried straight on. 'I presume you were landed sep-
arately somewhere on the south-east corner of the island,
especially as two of my sentries have disappeared in that
area. I am not asking, you notice. I am simply thinking
aloud.'

'Your privilege,' I told him.

'Allow me to continue, then. Your companions are in
uniform, you are in civilian clothes from which I deduce
that your task was to attempt to contact the local population for information.' He almost smiled, which for him
must have been quite a feat. 'There are exactly five islanders left here, Colonel Morgan, and I happen to know that
one way or another, they were all under surveillance last
night. You wasted your time, your men made a mess of
the business in the harbour and your gunboat, such a very
British term, I always think, is at the bottom of the sea.
Mission a failure.' He said those words in English. 'Isn't
that what they will stamp on the cover of the file?'

'Something like that.'

He straightened, placing his hands behind his back,
'You are familiar with the Kommandobefehl?'

'Naturally.'

'Then you will know that under its provisions, all members of the so-called commando units must be executed as
soon after capture as may be.'

'You're certainly taking your time about it.'

I didn't even strike a spark. He nodded gravely. 'As it
happens this action is the responsibility of the commanding officer in the particular area and I am not he, Colonel
Morgan. General Muller, the last governor, was killed by
a mine four weeks ago.'

'That was rather careless of him, wasn't it?'

'The new governor, Korvettenkapitan Karl Olbricht has
not yet arrived.'

'So you're just filling in?'

He permitted himself that wintry smile again. 'Something like that.'

'And I can expect to be shot only when the real governor flies in to sign the paper? What happens in the mean-
time?'

'You forfeit all privileges of rank.' It was at this point
that he sat down. 'You work, Colonel Morgan. There is
plenty of work for you here. You work in chains with the
rest of your companions.'

There didn't seem much point in quoting the Geneva Convention, but in any case, Steiner was speaking. 'I must again stress the gallant nature of Colonel Morgan's conduct this morning . . .'

'Which is noted, Steiner,' Radl said calmly. 'You are dismissed now.'

Steiner stayed where he was for a long moment while I prayed for him to get out of it. His face showed real emotion for the first time since I'd known him and he started to speak again.

Radl cut in on him again and gently, perhaps because of that Knight's Cross that hung from Steiner's neck, the one medal for valour they all respected, the one that meant the wearer shouldn't really be here.

'You are dismissed, Steiner.'

Steiner saluted, swung on heel and Radl said, 'You may take Colonel Morgan to join the others now, Brandt.'

'Hasn't anybody bothered to tell you how the war's going?' I said. 'In case they didn't, it's just about over and your side lost.'

Punctilious to the last, he saluted me gravely. I laughed in his face and walked out.

We drove up to Fort Edward on the point above Charlottestown. It was the largest of the four Victorian naval forts built in the eighteen-fifties during the period when the English government of the day was worried about its relations with France.

There was a sentry at the gate beside a machine gun in a sand-bagged emplacement and he waved us through the granite archway with Victoria Regina and the date 1856 carved above it.

Inside, grass grew between the cobbles which was nothing new, but several concrete gun emplacements were and there were trucks parked across the courtyard and a notice that indicated the presence of some kind of artillery unit. We got out of the field car and Brandt waved me on politely towards the wooden doors of the old blockhouse which stood open.

One of his police corporals hurried ahead and when we went inside, he had the leg irons ready. Brandt turned, face pale, and said in English, 'I am sorry, Colonel. A bad business, but a soldier's duty is to obey orders.'

'Get on with it, then,' I told him.

The corporal dropped to his knees and quickly snapped the steel collars around my ankles and tightened them with a screw key. The chain between was a little over two feet in length which allowed me to shuffle along at quite a reasonable rate.

'Where to now?' I demanded.

Brandt led the way without a word. We mounted the stone steps at the side of the blockhouse to the lower ramparts and walked towards the end of the point. As a boy of fourteen I had stood up there once a thousand years ago and watched the sea take my father. Now it was an artillery position and the walls were considerably knocked about, presumably by the naval bombardment of the previous year.

I could hear someone singing softly in German, a slow, sad old song from the first war. *Argonnerwald, Argonnerwald, a quiet graveyard now thou art*. We mounted to the second terrace and surprised a young sixteen year old masquerading as a soldier, who lounged beside an ammunition store, his rifle against the wall.

He jumped to attention rigidly and Brandt sighed and patted him gently on the head. 'One of these days, Durst, I will really have to put you on a charge.'

I liked him for that, which is something to be able to say about any kind of a military policeman. He unbolted the door and stood to one side. 'Colonel,' he said.

I moved in, the doors closed behind me. There was plenty of light in there from the old gun ports. Plenty of light and good sea air and rain pouring down the slimy walls. They were all waiting to greet me. Fitzgerald, Grant, Sergeant Hagen and Corporal Wallace. So Stevens and Lovat had been the unlucky ones, depending, of course, on how you looked at it.

'Christ Jesus, it's the colonel,' Hagen said.

Fitzgerald didn't seem to be able to think of anything to add to that and I smiled amiably at him. 'What was it your orders said. You will *Not* repeat *Not* attempt to land or provoke any incidents of a kind liable to alert the enemy to your presence. Enjoy yourself, did you?'

If he'd had a gun, he would have shot me dead, but all he did have was his fine aristocratic pride and it wasn't going to allow him to quarrel with riff-raff like me. He walked to the other end of the room and sat down.

Grant took a quick step towards me, those great hands

of his clenched, forgot his leg irons and fell on his knees.

'Now then, Sergeant,' I chided him. 'That's the trouble with you Rangers. No respect for rank.'

I scrambled up to the old gun platform. Rain drifted in a fine spray through the open ports and I produced my faithful waterproof tin, selected a cigarette, lit it and tossed the tin down to Hagen.

The view was really quite magnificent. On a good day it was possible to see Guernsey on the horizon thirty-five miles to the north-east, but not on a morning like this. And to the north-west, a hundred miles or more away across the Channel was the Cornish coast and Lizard Point where it had all started. *Four days ago.* It didn't seem possible.

1 The King of the First Four Hundred

The beach below the cottage on the cliffs two miles from Lizard Point, was blocked by the usual tangle of rusting barbed wire and the notice half-way down the track warned of mines.

It was an empty threat and something of a joke in the area, for the sergeant in charge of the operation, back in 1940, a local man, had seen little point in ruining one of the best surf fishing beaches in Cornwall.

It was thanks to this that I was able to swim from its white sands on that fine early April morning. It was unbelievably warm for the time of the year and the war had ceased to exist for me, was almost over anyway. I swam towards a spear of rock, climbed out and rested for a while.

Mary sat at her easel half-way along the beach, an old straw hat shading her from the sun, and painted the headland for what must have been the tenth time, although she argued that it always looked different, depending on her mood. She turned and looked out to sea searching for me, then waved. I waved back, dived in and started to swim for the shore.

She was waiting for me, a towel ready in one hand, my eye patch in the other. Not that my scarred face bothered her particularly. She had been a nurse too long for that, but she knew it still bothered me.

I dried my face, pulled on the patch and grinned.

'Marvellous out there. You should try it.'

'No thanks. Ask me again around July. I'll go up and see about lunch, Owen. Don't be long.'

She gave me a light kiss on the forehead and I watched her go through the wire and start up the path, aware of a kind of nostalgic affection and nothing more than that, which made me feel guilty on occasion.

We had met as students before the war and when they had carried me into that military hospital in Surrey five months previously pumped full of drugs and barely conscious, hers had been the first face I had seen on waking. Her husband had been killed in action, navigating a Lancaster in the Dresden raid. We had been living together for three months now, ever since my discharge from hospital.

I took my time about dressing, then walked across to the easel. She'd only got as far as the sketching stage with this one, but it was good—damned good. I picked up a piece of charcoal and tried a line or two myself, but without much success. Where perspective is concerned, two eyes are better than one and although I seemed to have adjusted in most things, I had a feeling that my painting days were over.

I lay down on the sand and pillowed my head in my hands, narrowing that one good eye to focus on a razor-bill that dropped through space for a perfect landing on the cliff face.

It was all so incredibly peaceful. Only the sea rushing in, the cry of a gull, a white cloud drifting. Who was I, then? Owen Morgan, sometime artist—of sorts. Novelist—very much so. Poet—debatable. Soldier, walker-in-darkness, hired bravo, cut-throat. It all depended on your point of view. And what was I doing caught in this pleasant limbo where one day eased into another and the horizon's rumble was thunder and not guns?

I must have slept, but only briefly. A gull cried harshly bringing me back to life. I was instantly awake, a habit hard come by in dark places, and got to my feet. If I didn't look sharp there would be Mary seeking me, the dinner burning and the devil to pay.

I went through the wire and started up the path, head down, I had barely reached the warning notice when a voice called, 'You down there!'

I glanced up, squinting into the sun and saw an American army officer standing on the brow of the hill, although who or what he was, it was impossible to say from that position with the sun behind him.

'I want a word with you,' he said.

It wasn't a request, but an order delivered in fine Bostonian tones, the kind of voice you get in New England and nowhere else in America and usually from a member of that happy little band whose ancestors stampeded to be first ashore from the *Mayflower*. I didn't like his voice and I didn't like him for all sorts of excellent reasons so I didn't bother to reply.

He spoke again with an edge of exasperation to his

voice. 'I am looking for Colonel Morgan. They told me at the house that he would be down on the beach. Have you seen him?'

Looking back on it now, I can find every excuse for him. He was gazing down on a small, dark man, badly in need of a shave and the old blue Guernsey sweater and the black eye patch didn't help. And neither, I suppose, did the gold ring I was wearing in my left ear at the insistence of Jack Trelawney, the landlord of the *Queen's Arms* up the road towards Falmouth, who believed implicitly that it would improve my sight and had pierced my ear lobe on one memorable evening with a darning needle and the assistance of half a bottle of pre-war Scotch.

He moved down out of the sun and close enough for me to see that he was a major by rank which wasn't surprising when one considered his medals. D.S.C. and Silver Star with Oak Leaf clusters for a second award which could mean everything or nothing. As someone once observed, only the man who holds an award knows what it is really worth and only the people who fought with him in the same battle can guess. On the other hand, when he came a little closer so that I could read the shoulder flash, I saw that he was a Ranger, and I'd always heard that there was little to choose between them and our own Commandos.

'Have you seen him?' he demanded patiently.

He was lovely. A sort of turn-of-the century American abroad having difficulty with the peasantry, straight out of the pages of Henry James.

'Well, now, that would be a difficult question to answer,' I answered in a fair to middling Cornish accent.

'You'd better buck your ideas up then, hadn't you?'

The hard Scots voice came as something of a surprise as did the hand that grabbed me by the shoulder and swung me round. Another Ranger, a master sergeant this time which made the Scots accent all the more intriguing. He had a raw, bony face and hard eyes that were swollen by the scar tissue of the prize fighter. A bad man to cross on a fine April morning.

'Come on, laddie, start trying a little harder,' he bellowed and shook me like a rat.

A good, tough soldier, just the man for a foray by night or a bridgehead landing under fire, but I had existed, survived for five years, in a world he had never known. A world where strength was not enough and courage was not enough. Where each new day came as a miracle. One survived, mainly by not caring whether one did or not.

I placed a hand on the hand that held me, twisted exactly as prescribed by a Japanese gentleman at a pleasant old country house in Surrey in the spring of 1940 and dropped to one knee. He rolled twenty feet down the hill into a gorse bush.

I looked up at the major and smiled gently. 'He made a mistake. Don't let him make another.'

He stared at me, puzzled, and then something clicked in his eyes. He knew then, I think, but before he could say anything, the master sergeant was coming back up the slope with the speed of a wounded bear. When he was about six feet away, my hand came out of my hip pocket holding the old spring-blade gutting knife I'd picked up on that first job back in Brittany in the second year of the war.

There was a nasty click when I pressed the button and the blade jumped into view. He stopped dead in his tracks, then crouched and started to move close.

'Grant, stay where you are! That's an order!' the major cut in crisply.

Grant still crouched, glaring at me, murder in his eyes and then another voice called, high and clear. 'Owen, for heaven's sake; what on earth's going on down there?'

The man who hurried down the track was in his sixties with snow-white hair, a long, rather ugly face and steel-rimmed spectacles. He wore an old Burberry and carried an umbrella and resembled to a remarkable degree the public image of an Oxford don. Which was exactly what he had been when we first met, although his talents had run to darker ends since those golden days.

I put up my knife and groaned. 'Oh, no, not you, Henry. Anything but that.'

Major Edward Arnold Fitzgerald and his Highland-American bully-boy moved stiffly away after Henry's formal introduction and I shook my head.

'The trouble with Fitzgerald's kind is that they can never take a man as they find him.'

Henry's eyebrows went up. 'But my dear Owen, that is precisely what he did do. Have you glanced in the mirror lately? I should have thought it unlikely that there is more than one half-colonel in His Majesty's service at the moment sporting a gold ring in his left ear.'

'You always did say I was an individualist,' I reminded him. 'How's the war going?'

'I understand the 1st Commando Brigade reached Luneburg yesterday.'

'They'll be thinking of crossing the Elbe next.'

He nodded. 'I expect so.'

We sat on an outcrop of rock and he produced a tin of a rather exotic Turkish cigarette he favoured and offered me one.

'You gave me one of those damned things the first time we met,' I said. 'Remember? The rough island boy up to Oxford for an education.'

He smiled faintly and with just a trace of sadness. 'A long time ago, Owen. A lot of water under the bridge.'

'And what will you do when it's all over?' I asked. 'Go back to being Henry Brandon, Fellow of All Souls, and everything that goes with it?'

He shrugged. 'One should never go back to anything, Owen. I don't think it's possible.'

'What you really mean is that you don't want to.'

'Do you?'

And as usual, with unfailing accuracy, he had touched the most tender spot of all.

'Go back to what?' I replied with some bitterness.

'Now don't start feeling sorry for yourself. It doesn't become you. I read this novel of yours the other day. I understand it's into its fourth printing in as many weeks. Remarkable.'

'Which means you didn't like it.'

'Does it matter? It must be making you a great deal of money.'

Which it was and for that I was duly grateful, and yet he had annoyed me, only vaguely perhaps, but enough to unsettle me.

He took a deep breath of good salt air and flung his arms wide.

'It's really quite beautiful, Owen. Quite beautiful. I envy you your life here—and I'm glad you and Mary Barton got together. You must have been very good for each other.'

And there was more than a grain of truth in that. During the six weeks in hospital when I couldn't see at all, I'd dictated my book to her, the one driving passion that had prevented me from going mad.

'I'm very grateful to Mary,' I said. 'I owe her more than I can ever repay.'

'But you don't love her?'

Once again he went straight to the heart of things with deadly accuracy and I stood up and flicked what was left of my cigarette over the edge of the cliff.

'All right, Henry, let's get down to it. What do you want?'

'It's quite simple really,' he said. 'We've got a job for you.'

I stared at him, thunderstruck, then laughed harshly. 'You've got to be joking. The war's over. It can't last more than another couple of months in Europe—you know that as well as I do.'

'On the mainland—yes, but the Channel Islands could prove to be something else again.'

I frowned and he held up a hand. 'No, let me explain. For some months now Naval Force 135 has been preparing Operation Nest Egg, the liberation of the Channel Islands, but it's an operation that is planned to take place only when the German garrison has surrendered. It's our hope that it will not be necessary for us to fight our way ashore. The results for the civilian population of the islands could be catastrophic.'

'And you think they might still try to hold out after defeat in Europe?'

'Let's put it this way. Vice-Admiral Huffmeier, the Commander in the Channel Islands, seems to show every intention of going down fighting. On the night of March the 8th he mounted a commando raid of his own and attacked Granville with two minesweepers. They destroyed three ships and a hell of a lot of dockside equipment into the bargain. When Doenitz congratulated him, Huffmeier signalled that he had every hope of being able to hang on in the Channel Islands for another year.'

'Could he be bluffing?'

Henry took off his spectacles and polished them carefully with his handkerchief. 'For years, Hitler has poured men and equipment into the islands. His great fear was that we might invade there first as a springboard to Europe.'

'So he was wrong. Doesn't that make them something of a dead letter?'

'The strongest fortifications in the world, Owen,' he said calmly. 'The same number of strong points and batteries as they had to defend the entire European coast from Dieppe to St Nazaire. Add to that a garrison of something like forty thousand troops and you'll see what I mean.'

'So what am I supposed to do about it?'

'Go home, Owen,' he said. 'Go back to St Pierre. I'd have thought you would have enjoyed that.'

2 Now Destroy

St Pierre is the most outlying of the Channel Islands and fourth in size. During the eighteen-fifties the British Government, alarmed by the development by the French of a strong naval base at Cherbourg, embarked on a plan which was designed to make Alderney into the Gibraltar of the North. Most of the workers imported to labour on the fortifications were Irish fleeing the effects of the famine in their unhappy country.

A similar scheme, though on a less ambitious scale, was mounted in St Pierre. A breakwater was constructed to enlarge the harbour at Charlottestown and four naval forts were built at various points on the coast.

The labour force, so far as St Pierre was concerned, was imported from South Wales which explains that strange mixture of Welsh and French and English to be found on the island and accounts for the fact that my father, and I following him, had a name like Owen Morgan although my mother, God rest her soul, had been born Antoinette Rozel and spoke French for preference to me until the day she died.

Standing there now on the Lizard cliffs, I stared out to sea south-west to Brittany beyond the horizon, to the Golfe de St Malo and St Pierre and for the briefest of moments, a fugue in time, I saw the grey-green island again, those granite cliffs splashed with bird lime, sea birds crying, wheeling in great clouds, razorbills, shags, gulls, oyster-catchers and my own especial favourite, the storm petrel. And there was laughter, too, faintly on the wind and I seemed to see again a young girl, skin browned by summer's heat, long hair flying as she ran from the barefoot fisher boy. *Simone.* I could almost reach out and touch her.

Instead, a hand on the arm brought me back to life. I turned and found Henry at my side, a slight, quizzical frown on his face. 'Will you go, Owen?'

For five and a half years I had done this man's bidding, had lived in constant danger of my life, had lied, cheated, killed, murdered, until my very nature seemed to have changed. After that final bloody business in the Vosges Mountains, the eight-day battle with crack S.S. fighting troops that had left me maimed for life, I had thought such days over, gone for ever. And now, my heart was beginning to pound, my throat to go dry.

'I'm going to tell you something, Henry,' I said, and when I lit a cigarette, my hands were trembling. 'I've been lying here in the sun for some considerable time now, trying to write and failing, trying to love one of the finest women I've met in my life and failing at that also. I've got a good friend up the road who supplies me with all the pre-war Scotch I can drink, but I seem to have lost my taste for it. I slept better on the run in France, in the blackest days of '41, than I do now. Would you say that any of that made any kind of sense at all?'

'My dear Owen, it's quite simple. You enjoyed every single minute of it. Walking the knife-edge between life and death was meat and drink to you. You have lived more in one day working for me, really lived with action and passion as a man should, than you could have in a lifetime of writing bad poetry and popular novels. That's why you will go to St Pierre now. Because you need to go. Because you want to go.'

And at that he had miscalculated, had gone too far and I shook my head. 'Like hell, I will, Henry, and there's damn all you can do about it.' I tapped my eye patch. 'Medically unfit for further service. You even got me a civil list pension. Send our American friend. It's more his style.'

He produced a buff envelope from his inside pocket, took out a letter and handed it to me. 'I hope you'll find that explicit enough. When I discussed it with him, I did

point out that there was always the possibility you might
feel you'd done your share.'

The letter was from Downing Street, hand-written and
bore the usual signature. It informed me that I was returned to the active list forthwith and must consider myself to be under the order of Section D and Professor
Henry Brandon in connection with operation GRANDE
PIERRE. A nice touch that for Grand Pierre had been
my field name in Vosges. The letter was stamped *Action
this day.*

So that was very much that. I held the letter up. 'The
first personal one he ever sent me. Can I have it?'

He took it from my fingers. 'Afterwards, Owen, when
you come back.'

I nodded and sat down on the rock beside him again.
'All right, Henry, you'd better tell me about it.'

'According to our information, the island's been reasonably heavily fortified,' Henry said. 'There was at one time
a garrison of something like sixteen hundred, but during
the last couple of years, it's been drastically reduced. The
airstrip never amounted to much and after it had been
bombed half-a-dozen times, they abandoned it and withdrew the Luftwaffe personnel.'

'What about the Navy?'

'They tried to use it as an E-boat base for a while, but
it never really worked out. I don't need to tell you how
dangerous those waters are and the tides are a law unto
themselves. Plenty of times the harbour is completely un-
usable so the Navy pulled out as well, although they use it
on occasion. That left mainly Artillery units and Pioneers.'

'How many now?'

'We think six hundred. Mainly old men and young
boys. Things have changed since that glorious romp
through France in 1940.'

'How many islanders?'

'Apparently you can pretty well count them on the fingers of one hand. Most of the population, as you know,
chose to be evacuated to England in 1940 just before the
occupation.'

'Sixty or so stayed,' I said. 'Including the Seigneur and
his daughter.'

'Ah yes, Henri de Beaumarchais. He's dead, it seems. Killed in the naval bombardment.'

I stared at him blankly not quite taking it in. 'Dead—Henri de Beaumarchais? What naval bombardment?'

'Ours last year. They had a go at the harbour from three miles out. His daughter is apparently still there, but almost everyone else was moved out six months back. I'm really not quite sure why she hasn't gone with the others, but there it is.'

'She will be Seigneur now,' I said. 'Lord of St Pierre. They had a woman once before, back in the thirteenth century. She used the male title. Simone will do the same. She has a great respect for tradition.'

I thought of her a moment, out there beyond the horizon in the old manor house that had been the Seigneurie for untold generations. It had been a long war. She must have been lonely. Lonelier still, now that her father was gone.

It was almost five years since I had seen her. On a dark night in July, 1940, to be precise, a fortnight after the German occupation of the Channel Islands. I had gone in by submarine and landed from a rubber boat at La Grande Bay at the eastern end of the island. It had been as abortive a business as most similar exploits were at that time. I'd see Simone and her father at the Seigneurie and discovered there were no more than two hundred Germans on the island. I was to be picked up a couple of hours before dawn and had begged them to come with me. They had refused, as I had known in my heart they would, but Simone had insisted on accompanying me to the beach. I remembered that now, and her face a pale blur in the darkness.

'The thing is,' Henry said, 'we're losing rather a lot of ships in the Channel area, starting six months ago. The same time most of the remaining population was evacuated, you'll notice. Quite a shock when we discovered what it was.'

'Secret weapons at this stage in the war?'

'Good God, no. We knew about this thing as long ago as Anzio. The Germans were late getting into the underwater sabotage field of things with frogmen and so on. Rather surprising when you consider the Italians really started it all. Anyway, they did come up with a lethal little item called Nigger which they used with some success at Anzio.'

'And now they're trying it in the Channel?'

'That's about the size of it. All they've done is take a normal torpedo, scoop out the warhead and fix controls. There's a glass cupola to protect the operator who sits astride the thing with a live torpedo slung underneath. The general idea is to point it at the target, release the second torpedo at the last minute and try to swerve out of the way.'

'And where did they get the men to play that kind of game?'

'The Brandenberg Division mainly. They seem to have provided the nearest thing the Germans have to our own Commandos. Some are survivors of Otto Skorzeny's Danube group. Those frogmen of his gave the Russians hell up there.'

'And you think they're operating from St Pierre?'

'Until three weeks ago at least.'

'You're certain of that?'

'We've got someone who was there until then who says so. A man called Joseph St Martin. Turned up on the French coast near Granville in an open boat. Says he knows you.'

'Oh yes, he knows me all right.' I touched the bridge of my nose gently where the bone showed crooked. 'He broke this for me when I was fifteen.'

'Did he then?' Henry said softly. 'As a matter of interest, I've got him up at the house now.'

I frowned. 'You're moving fast aren't you?'

'No other choice. You must go in the day after tomorrow. The Navy tell me that if we miss that particular tide, conditions won't be right for another three weeks.'

'Let me get this straight. The general purpose of this affair is for me to get ashore, find out as much as I can about the Nigger operation and get off again, presumably during the same night?'

'That's about the size of it. I'm hoping the information St Martin can give you will help you to find your way about. There are still people on the island you could contact. Miss de Beaumarchais, for example.'

I sat there frowning as I tried to take it all in. 'And you really think that this is important, Henry, at this stage in the war?'

He held up the famous letter. 'The Government evidently does. If the Germans decide to fight in the Channel Islands instead of surrendering, this Nigger installation could wreak havoc with the ships of any invading Force.'

'And what about Fitzgerald? Where does he fit in?'

'He's a good man, Owen. Decorated three times. He's been on the staff of the 21st Specialist Service Raiding Force for the past couple of years. They're a mixed bunch. American Rangers, French and British Commandos. They specialise in small boat work, underwater sabotage and so on. Fitzgerald has raided across the Channel on twenty-three separate occasions.'

'Are you including the time they blew up the empty lighthouse in Brittany and all those landings on uninhabited islands off the French coast and deserted beaches where they never saw a soul and no one saw them or was that another unit?'

'Now you're being bitter again.'

'Oh, don't get me wrong. I've as much respect for the genuine Commando units as anyone. Those boys who just hacked their way through to Luneberg yesterday, for instance, but outfits like Fitzgerald's are something else again. The nearest thing to private armies we've had since the Middle Ages, living off the fat of the land and operating out of country houses. Put them all together and what have most of these special service units really achieved?'

He smiled. 'Well, for one thing, they've provided employment for some very awkward customers.'

'Like the King of the first four hundred?' I shook my head. 'The family must be proud of him, fruit salad and all and still time for his Medal of Honour, don't forget that. All right, tell me the worst. What's he supposed to do?'

And I couldn't believe my ears when he did tell me. Fitzgerald and five companions were to enter the harbour at Charlottestown in two-man Rob Roy canoes. The intention was to fix limpet mines on everything in sight and to get out again without being discovered.

'For God's sake, Henry, what's the point? It's raiding for raiding's sake,' I said when he'd finished. 'They'll be lucky if there's anything in the harbour worth bothering with.'

'Perhaps so and you're entitled to think that if you want, but let me make one thing clear. Originally this wasn't our party. Combined Operations are behind it. I only heard about it quite by chance and made immediate representation through channels. I thought of you, naturally, and your unique knowledge of the island and persuaded them to modify their plan.'

'Well that was nice of you. May I ask who's in command?'

'You are by virtue of seniority, but no situation is likely to arise in which you would need to exercise such authority. You will land alone and will have your own task to perform. Major Fitzgerald and his men will look after themselves.'

'As long as he doesn't start to hear bugles blowing faintly on the wind,' I said. 'He looks the kind who wants to die, sabre in hand, trailing clouds of glory if you ask me.'

'Oh, I think he'll be sensible. No intelligent man would want to put his head on the block at this stage in the war, would he?'

I laughed out loud—couldn't help it. 'Your sense of irony always was one of your most endearing traits, Henry.'

'Good, it's nice to see you smiling again.' He stood up and rubbed his hands together. 'And now for a spot of the excellent lunch Mrs Barton and your daily were preparing when I was up there. She gave us forty minutes.'

'Not me.' I shook my head. 'I'll stay down here for a while, I want to think. One thing you can do—send down Joe St Martin. I might as well get that side of it over. He was never one of my favourite people.'

'All right, Owen.' He appeared to hesitate and had the grace to look ever so slightly ashamed as he took another buff envelope from his pocket. 'You might as well have your D-Section *Operation Order*.'

I took it from him. 'Made out in advance I see.'

'I'm afraid so.'

'Enjoy your dinner, Henry.' I watched him go up the track and disappear over the brow of the hill before opening the envelope. Inside was a typical D Section *Operation Order*, the entire business reduced to sparse Civil Service English.

Operation Instruction No. D 103
For Lieutenant-Colonel Owen Morgan.
Operation: GRANDE PIERRE
Field Name: Not necessary.

INFORMATION—Phase 1.

We have discussed with you the possibility of your
landing on the island of St Pierre in the Channel Islands to obtain as much information as possible re-
garding the scope of the enemy project noted in files
as NIGGER. You have made it clear that in your
view, nothing prevents you from returning to this island which was originally your home.

We feel that information provided by Joseph St
Martin should make it relatively easy for you to get
in touch with sources on the island from which the
information you seek may be readily available.

INFORMATION—Phase 2.

During the time that you are on the island, Major
Edward Fitzgerald, Master Sergeant Grant, Sergeant
Hagen, Corporals Wallace, Stevens and Lovat, will
enter the main harbour at Charlottestown in three
Rob Roy canoes with the intention of fixing limpet
mines to any vessels they can find. This is the sole
purpose of their mission and they must NOT repeat
NOT attempt to land or provoke any incidents of a
kind liable to alert the enemy to their presence.

In any circumstances calling for a drastic re-ap-
praisal of the situation, you, as senior officer, are
considered to be in command.

METHOD

It is our information that under the provisions of
Hitler's Kommandobefehl, special service troops falling into enemy hands are still being executed, but we
also know of instances where they have simply been
put to work in chains. On balance, therefore, if captured, there is a better chance for survival as a soldier than as a spy. For this reason we have decided,
in this instance, not to give you a cover story. You
will use your own name and rank and identity discs
will be provided.

You will be taken to St Pierre on the night of the 25th on MGB 109LT and off-loaded by surf boat at approx. 22.30 hours. Major Fitzgerald and party will be off-loaded half a mile off the harbour entrance at 23.00 hours.

You MUST repeat MUST be picked up first at approximately 02.00 hours and the other party will rendezvous as soon as may be with the MGB after that.

INTERCOMMUNICATIONS
There will be no W|T communication whatsoever. Hand-lamp signals only to be used during pick-up.

WEAPONS
At your discretion, but only that which you consider essential for hand-to-hand combat.

CONCLUSION
You have been sufficiently familiarised with the situation to realise the importance of this mission. Nothing should be allowed to prevent you from obtaining the information you are seeking and if the situation should warrant it, your own mission MUST repeat MUST take precedence over that of Major Fitzgerald's to the extent of abandoning him and his men if necessary.
NOW DESTROY . . . NOW DESTROY . . . NOW DESTROY . . . NOW DESTROY

I struck a match, held it to one corner of the sheet and let it burn. It drifted to the ground and I stamped it to ashes, grinding it into the grass with my heel, then I went back down the track to the beach.

It was plain enough, including the juicy item about the Kommandobefehl, not that it bothered me particularly. My only question for the past five years had not been *would* they kill me when they got their hands on me, but how. For a memorable two days at Gestapo headquarters at II rue de Saussaies, at the back of the Ministry of the Interior in Paris, I had thought my time was up but I'd played small fish and they'd fallen for it. Two days later, I'd jumped from a train taking me to Poland to labour for

the Todt Organisation along with thousands of other poor
wretches.

I went down through the wire and walked along the
sand to the water's edge, thinking about it all, but mainly
about Simone out there across the sea, alone in the old
house in the hollow among the beech trees lonely from
the beginning of time until now.

The line circled in my brain, no end to it. *Lonely from
the beginning of time until now*. It was from a poem she
was particularly fond of. Chinese originally and translated
by Ezra Pound. *By the North gate the wind blows full of
sand*. I stared out to sea, my heart and brain filled with
memories of her and someone called out behind me.

Joe St Martin stood on the far side of the wire and
waited and I called to him. 'You've nothing to worry
about—come on.'

He came reluctantly, treading on eggs for the first few
yards, then seemed to get his confidence back all at once
and came on at a quickened pace. He had five years on
me, which would make him thirty-one or -two now, a big,
boastful ox of a man. I'd disliked him all my life and he,
in his turn, had always had a strange kind of contempt for
me. Little Owen—Little Owen Morgan, that's what he had
called me, his fingers twisted into my hair. *Dance for us,
then, little black pig*. The Welsh side of him coming out
in the famous old song.

And then, when I was fifteen, I caught him up on the
top meadow, rolling in the hay with Simone who was
doing her level best to put his eyes out. I hit him with everything I had and got a broken nose for my pains. Not a
very gallant showing, but when he had gone, she cried
over me and kissed me for the first time, which seemed to
make up for everything. She was seventeen then, two
years older than me and at that age it can seem an insur-
mountable gap normally, but from then on there was no
one else in the world for either of us.

He was wearing a blue serge suit a size too large, a
white polo neck sweater and army boots and the combination somehow made him seem clumsy and uncouth. He
was frowning uncertainly and paused about five yards
away. 'Owen, is that you?' I didn't say a word and he
shook his head in a kind of wonder. 'A colonel they tell
me you are.'

'That's right,' I said.

He grinned suddenly, the same old familiar leering grin. 'Little Owen—little Owen Morgan. I'd never have recognised you.'

'Dance for us little black pig.'

The smile left his face and he stared blankly. 'What's that?'

'Never mind,' I said. 'They tell me you were on the island till three weeks ago. Tell me about it.'

'Not much to tell.' He shrugged. 'I saw my chance of skipping in a fishing boat and took it. I knew most of Britany was in Allied hands now, see?'

'How did you know?'

'Ezra told me, Ezra Scully. Kept his radio right through the occupation. Listened to the B.B.C. regular.'

'I understand that most of the locals were moved to Guernsey six months ago?'

'That's right. It was after they went that the frogmen moved in.'

'Why were you kept on?'

He shrugged. 'They needed a couple of pilots for the harbour and the passage. You know what Le Coursier can be like. They was always losing boats, see.'

'So they kept you and Ezra?'

'That's it.'

'Who else?'

'Jethro Hughes is still on his farm with his son, Justin. The Jerries need milk, just like anyone else. And old Doctor Riley—they've kept him 'cause they don't have enough Army doctors to go round.'

'And the Seigneur?'

'Killed in the shelling last year, but she's still there—Simone. She's Seigneur now.'

'Is that why they've allowed her to stay? Because she's Seigneur?'

'Maybe, I don't know.' He shrugged. 'Whore would be a better name for her, her and her fancy man, Steiner. Seigneur? Jerrybag more like.'

My own voice, when I answered him, seemed to belong to someone else, to come from outside of me. 'What are you talking about?'

'Simone—Simone and this fancy man of hers—Steiner. A sergeant-major, that's all he is, but they treat him like he was the Fuhrer himself.'

'You're lying,' I said.

'Lying, is it? I've seen them plenty of times, I can tell you, and her posing for him with nothing on and there's a sight for you, believe me.' And then he remembered and a slow, sly grin seeped across his face. 'I was forgetting, wasn't I? You was sweet on her. Poor Owen—poor little Owen Morgan. You'd like to have a go at her yourself, eh? And I don't blame you, boyo. By God, I could give her something to remember.' He started to laugh and gave me the same old half-contemptuous dig in the shoulder I remembered so well from boyhood.

I slapped him hard across the face and my voice, when I spoke, was my own again. 'People don't really change Joe, do they? You always had a foul mouth.'

He touched his face in astonishment, a kind of wonder there and then rage broke through like hot lava bubbling to the surface. He came in with a rush, intent on the kind of beating he had been fond of handing out in the old days.

But times had changed and if he hadn't, Owen Morgan had. I didn't give him any kind of chance. My right foot caught him in the groin, a blow that could have crippled him for life had I not been wearing rope-soled beach sandals. He doubled over with a cry and my knee lifted into his face, straightening him again.

He lay on his back, knees up, writhing in agony and I squatted beside him. 'Don't look now, Joe, but I seem to have broken your nose.'

He glared up at me, hating still through the pain and I got to my feet, turned and found Master Sergeant Grant standing on the other side of the wire. When I got close enough, he sprang to attention. 'The lady sent me down, Colonel. She says if you want to eat, you'd better come now.'

'Fair enough,' I nodded towards St Martin who was sitting up, both hands between his thighs. 'Stay with our friend there till he can walk, then bring him up. We've still some talking to do.'

His hand flicked up in a superb salute, his iron face showed nothing as he turned and went through the wire. I left him to it and started up the path.

I paused half-way, my heart pounding, but not from fatigue. Was it true? Could it possibly be true? No, I could never believe it—never. Hatred for Joe St Martin rose like

bile into my mouth. I think if I had gone back to the
beach I might have killed him then, for the black Celtic
rage that was a heritage of the Welsh side of me took pos-
session as it had done before on occasions of great stress.
It required a real physical effort to keep me climbing up
the track towards the house.

3   A Man Called Steiner

I suppose the most obvious difference between Fitzgerald
and myself was to be found in the fact that my father had
been born in a two-roomed cottage and had earned his
living, at least in the beginning, as an inshore fisherman
whereas Fitzgerald was the son of one of the richest mer-
chant bankers in America and would one day succeed
him. Handicap enough for any man if you added to it all
that New England tradition. Looking back on it all now, I
see that I should have been kinder to him, but a man is
what he is, moulded by everything that has ever happened
to him and change is difficult. Fitzgerald was branded in a
way that only the very rich can be so that even Princeton
must have been superfluous and I was a black little
Welsh-Breton peasant in spite of my father's money and
Oxford and far too handy with a knife for the kind of
gentleman who thought it was sporting to stand up like a
man to have his face pulped by someone who could box
better than he.

I took the knife out now, sprung the blade and threw it
underhand all in one quick fluid movement. It quivered
gently in the wooden post at the end of the verandah five
feet above the ground.

I grinned at Henry as I went to retrieve it. 'And I'd lay
you odds I'm the only half-colonel in the British Army
who can do that.'

Fitzgerald was sitting on the verandah rail, drinking his
coffee. He cleared his throat. 'Rather more difficult in the
dark, sir, which after all is when one is more likely to
want to use a trick like that. You know the sort of
thing—night landing and sentry on the cliffs. We used to
practice with our eyes blindfolded at the Commando Depot at Achnacarry. Remember, Sergeant Grant?'

Grant had been playing batman and stood at ease by the door. 'I don't recall anyone being much better at it than you, sir,' he said dutifully.

It was a challenge of sorts and I took it, but for my own dark reasons. I knew he could do it before he made the attempt, for he was not the sort of man to accept failure of the public variety at anything he put his hand to.

He weighed the knife in his right hand for a moment, then closed his eyes and threw it by the blade with such force that the point buried itself two inches into the wood.

He opened his eyes and smiled blankly. 'Ah, good.'

I retrieved the knife, folded it and shook my head. 'As a gambling friend of mine used to say, never play against a winning streak.' There was something close to uncertainty in his eyes, and then a kind of contempt. 'But you've definitely earned yourself a very large Scotch, Major,' I added. 'If you'd like to go inside, you'll find all you need in the parlour.'

He frowned and glanced at Henry. 'May I ask when we may expect to get down to the business of the day, Professor Brandon?'

'When I'm ready, Major Fitzgerald,' I cut in brightly, 'you'll be the first to know.'

I thought he might blow then, but he simply turned on heel and walked away stiffly followed by Grant.

Henry didn't say a word, so I walked to the far end of the verandah, closed my eyes, pulled out the knife, turned and threw it. It hit the post no more than an inch from the first mark.

'Satisfied?' I demanded.

He sighed and went to retrieve it for me. 'Circus tricks, Owen. Schoolboy games.'

'Three months, Henry, three months of my life I spent learning to do that on that farm in Brittany with my left leg in splints. The autumn of 1940. As I recall rather vividly, parachute packing wasn't all that it might have been in those days.'

'What are you playing at, Owen? Why ride Fitzgerald so hard?'

'Because it pleases me—because I feel like it. If you don't approve, you could always find somebody else.'

He wasn't smiling any longer, even that perpetual, sardonic little quirk of his was missing for the first time since I'd known him.

'What is it, Owen? What's wrong?'

I held up the knife. 'Schoolboy games, Henry? To you perhaps, sitting behind that desk of yours scheming and planning, paper all the way. I've killed five times with this little item. Give that a thought sometime when you're having your tea break.' I snapped the knife shut and slipped it back into my pocket. 'I'll see St Martin now and I'd like you to stay.'

He left, white-faced, and I opened the cupboard under the box seat and found half-a-bottle of Scotch and an enamel mug that didn't look any too clean, but I'd drunk from stranger vessels than that in my time. The whisky burned through to the bone and I had another.

I was sitting on the verandah rail lighting a cigarette when Henry appeared with St Martin. He looked pale and ill, a good ten years older than when I'd last seen him and there was hatred in his eyes. If I'd paid heed to it I suppose things might have turned out differently, but then, you can never be certain of anything in this life.

I poured some whisky into the mug and handed it to him. He took it without a word and I asked Henry to get the maps. There was an Admiralty chart of the general area of the Golfe de St Malo and a pre-war ordnance survey map of St Pierre. A certain amount of information had been added to it in indian ink: gun installations, strong points and the like, presumably obtained from St Martin. I pulled the wicker chair forward to the table and motioned him into it. 'I'm going to ask you some questions now and I want clear and accurate answers. Understand?'

He nodded and we went to work. Mostly, he was simply confirming what Henry had already told me, but we covered everything step-by-step because I wanted to know exactly what I was getting into.

The picture which emerged was a reasonably gloomy one. All beaches were mined which was only to be expected and a landing of any sort seemed impossible, which was already indicated by the information on the map.

'Only one place I can think of.' He stabbed his fingers at the peninsula that jutted into the sea in the south-east corner of the island.

'The Devil's Staircase?'

'You could do it if the tide was right and it ought to be.'

'But the cliffs must be three hundred feet high at that point,' Henry said.

St Martin nodded. 'That's why they haven't any defences there. Don't reckon to need none.'

'And they don't know about the Devil's Staircase?'

He shook his head. 'If they did, I'd have known for sure.'

I explained quickly to Henry. 'At low tide it wouldn't be possible, but a twenty-five-foot rise puts you level with a hole in the cliff face that takes you into a fissure going all the way up.'

'I must say it still sounds something of a performance,' he observed.

'I've done it before.'

'In daylight, presumably?'

I shrugged that one off and moved on to discuss the exact location of each of the civilians still left on the island. Doctor Riley was living in the town and Ezra Scully still resided in his old cottage by the lifeboat station at Granville on the south side of the island.

'Don't know how he does it,' St Martin said. 'All on his own like that. The other cottages at Granville have stood empty since 1940.'

'Jethro Hughes and son—they'll still be at the Manor Farm?' He nodded and I went on, 'And Miss de Beaumarchais?'

'At the Seigneurie—at the Manor House as always.'

Which surprised me, but I was on dangerous ground here and I think he knew it. I contented myself with asking whether she had anyone billeted on her.

He shook his head. 'No, her father wouldn't have that. Insisted on his rights as Seigneur and the Jerries met him more than half-way. They didn't want any trouble, see? After the old man was killed they offered her a cottage in town, but she refused.'

I left it at that. 'What about the frogmen?'

'They moved in about five months ago after most of the islanders had gone to Guernsey. There was thirty of them when they first came.'

'Who was in charge?'

'A young lieutenant called Braun was supposed to be, but he was drowned second week there, not that he ever counted for much. It was Steiner all the way from the first—Sergeant-Major Steiner!'

I could feel the hollowness inside me, the coldness uncoiling and poured myself another drink. 'Tell me about him.'

'What do you want to know?' I think it was then that I realised he hadn't liked Steiner at all, which was something in the German's favour. 'You takes your pick with him. Even the governor, the old general, used to treat him with kid gloves and he was S.S.'

'What is so special about him?'

'I don't know. To start with he just doesn't give a damn for anyone. Spends half his time sketching and painting all over the island and speaks English better than you do. One of the Pioneer corporals once told me that he'd been to college in London, and that his father—no, his stepfather, that was it—was a big man back home.'

I turned to Henry who was already opening his briefcase. 'We checked all the London Art Colleges. There was a Manfred Steiner at the Slade from 1935-37. We managed to trace a couple of his tutors with very little difficulty.' He produced a paper. 'Do you want to read it?'

I shook my head. 'Tell me.'

'He was born in 1916 and his father was killed in the last year of the war. Prussian family—the kind who usually go into the Army. His mother married again when he was ten. A man called Otto Furst.'

'Furst the industrial? The arms manufacturer?'

'That's him.'

'Do you think Steiner could have been working as a spy, amateur variety before the war?' I asked. 'Plenty of these so-called students were.'

'I don't know.' He shook his head. 'It's this sergeant-major thing that I find so puzzling.'

And he was right. Considering Steiner's background, it was all wrong, but there was little to be gained from any further discussion and I moved on to other things.

The governor, old General Muller, had been killed in some kind of accident about a week before St Martin had fled, which had left his chief aide, an S.S. Colonel called Radl, as acting governor. St Martin had plenty to say about him, the word swine figuring largely in his description which left me with the distinct impression that Colonel Radl was a hard man.

I made a few notes on the map, stared at it speculatively for a moment then nodded, 'All right, that'll do me, Henry. Get rid of him.'

Joe St Martin got to his feet and leaned heavily on the table, his eyes wild. 'I hope they get you, Owen Morgan. I hope they leave you hanging on the wire for the gulls to finish off.'

'It's certainly a thought,' I said and went back into the house, taking the maps with me.

I could hear voices as I approached the parlour, the door being ajar, Grant was speaking in the kind of voice senior N.C.O.s in the Guards Brigade keep for those few occasions when they find themselves on some kind of social footing with one of their own senior officers. Good hearty man-to-man stuff with just the right touch of deference from someone who knows his place.

'Funny kind of set-up, sir,' he was saying. 'Colonel Morgan.' There was just the right small laugh, nicely judged. 'Well, sir, not like the old days when I was in the Scots Guards, I can tell you. He wouldn't have fitted in at all.'

He had made a very bad mistake. Fitzgerald's voice was like icewater. 'Grant, if I ever hear you discuss Colonel Morgan or any other officer in those terms again in my hearing, I'll break you, understand? Now get out of here and wait for me in the car.'

'Sir!' Grant's voice rebounded from the walls and I could picture the salute as his foot stamped in hard. He came through the door, swerved to one side and saluted me on the way past. It was all very un-American.

Fitzgerald was standing at the window, and turned as I entered. 'Did you find the Scotch all right?' I asked as I spread the maps on the table.

'Indeed I did, sir.' He came forward, his swagger stick under one arm, hands behind his back.

I went to the sideboard and opened a bottle. 'Care for another?'

'No thank you.'

'Suit yourself. How does a Highland Scot come to be in the American Army?'

'Grant?' He shrugged. 'He was a regular soldier in your own Army for a while—Scots Guards. Bought himself out and turned prizefighter. Took out American nationality just before the war.'

'Is he any good?'

It was as if I'd made an improper suggestion. 'A first-rate fighting man,' he said, a touch of indignation in his voice.

'All right no need to get emotional about it.' I half-filled a tumbler and carried it over to the table as Henry appeared. 'Right, let's get down to it! I'll have a look at your orders now, Major.'

He produced them without a murmur and I read them through briefly. They closely resembled my own and particularly stressed the really important things. That my mission was to take precedence over his, that on no account was he to land or look for unnecessary trouble and that in any extreme situation he was to turn to me for orders.

'You've read this thoroughly and understand it?'

He nodded. 'Perfectly.'

I dropped it into the fire and returned to the chart and the map. 'I know these waters like the back of my hand, Major, which is rather important because they're a death trap and the orders you've been given would have very probably been the end of you and your men.'

Henry stared at me in astonishment, but Fitzgerald took it rather well and waited patiently for me to continue. 'On completion of your mission, you're supposed to leave the harbour, paddle due east one mile and signal for the pickup.'

'That's right.'

I shook my head. 'If you do, they'll wait all night and never see you.' I ran my finger along the water off the northern edge of the island. 'See that, Major, Le Coursier—the Mill-Race. A hell of a place at the best of times, but when the tide starts to ebb, you'll get a ten knot current that'll take your light canoes in its grip and never let go until it smashes you to a pulp against the cliffs on the east coast!'

'I see.' He nodded gravely. 'What would you suggest as an alternative?'

'Once out of harbour, turn south round Fort Windsor, then follow the coastline till you come to here.' I tapped the spot with my finger. 'Which is where I'm being picked up.'

Fitzgerald examined the map for a moment. 'I'd say it's an improvement. We'll save time on the pick-up all round.'

'That's settled then.' I folded the maps and gave them

to Henry. 'All yours, Henry. When do you want me to come up to town?'

'No need for that, Owen. Falmouth tomorrow night. I'll send a car. You'll leave at noon the following day.'

'That suits me. The sooner the better now that we know what we're doing.'

'Good, I think that's everything.' Henry put the maps into his brief-case. 'We'll be off. I'll just make my fare-wells to Mrs Barton.'

He moved out and Fitzgerald started to follow, then hesitated, strangely awkward. 'I hope you don't mind me asking, but the painting above the fireplace there. It really is quite extraordinary, but I couldn't make a great deal of sense out of the signature.'

'You wouldn't,' I said. 'It's in Welsh. An affectation of the painter.'

'I see. It's remarkable—quite remarkable. If there was ever any chance that you were considering selling . . .'

I looked up into the steady grey eyes of the woman in the picture and she seemed to be about to speak to me as she always did. I shook my head. 'I hardly think so. I'm glad you like it though. It's a painting of my mother done the month before my father was killed. The best thing he ever did which is saying a great deal, Major Fitzgerald.'

There was a silence that for some reason, grated on me. It occurred to me that he was perhaps attempting to make some kind of gesture. I know now that I misjudged him badly.

'Just one thing before you go,' I said. 'No boy scout stuff on this one, no fancy heroics. You've got all the me-dals you'll ever need to impress them back home.'

His face went very pale for a moment, there was some-thing like pain in his eyes. He took a deep breath, adjus-ted his forage cap and saluted formally.

'May I have the colonel's permission to leave?'

'Oh, go on, damn you, get out of it!' I said sourly and he saluted again, face grave and left.

I could imagine now how Burgoyne must have felt at Saratoga.

I was in no mood to face Mary after that and went out quietly through the garden. I spent the afternoon walking rather aimlessly along the cliffs, thinking about it all and didn't return to the house till early evening.

There was no sign of her and I went out to the verandah. The sky was every shade of flame, orange and purple, the sun dropping vast beyond the rim of the world and there was silence as dusk fell, everything black, etched against flame.

Ravens, seven of them perched on the roof of the old summer-house. A sign, surely, a portent, but of what, I could not be sure. That was the writer in me, the part of me that wanted things to happen for a reason, to have a sequence to them, some meaning.

There was a stirring in the darkness and Mary said, 'Can you tell me about it?'

'I'm going back into harness. St Pierre, the day after tomorrow.'

She was genuinely shocked. 'But this is nonsense—absolute nonsense. The war is virtually over. Why should Henry expect you to stick your head in a noose at this stage? You've done enough. More than enough.'

'There's a lot to it.' I said and gave her the brief details, or as much as she needed to know. 'You're the only person in the world I'd tell and only because I owe you some sort of explanation.'

'You owe me nothing.' She put a hand to my face. 'I helped you, but you helped me, Owen. I can go on from here in a way I couldn't before. No lies, no commitment, just as we agreed.'

'Fair enough.' The relief, from guilt, was almost physical. 'What about some supper?'

'All right.' She moved to the door and paused. 'Owen, I know you're acting under orders, but the truth is, you want to go, don't you?'

'I'm honestly not sure.'

She shook her head. 'Poor Owen, what will you do when it's all over? What will you do when there's an end to killing?'

At least she had assumed I would survive, which was something.

4 A Fast Boat and a Passage by Night

After that first abortive mission to St Pierre in July, 1940, Henry had put me in for parachute training, if that's the word. A group of us had shivered in the cold morning air of a rather desolate and windswept Yorkshire airport and watched sandbags being parachuted from a twin-engined Whitley. Any confidence we might have had in man's ability to overcome the forces of nature was soon dispelled by the fact that at least half the parachutes didn't open.

A fortnight and five jumps later, I plunged through the hole that had been specially fitted in the floor of the Whitley for just that purpose, and found myself dropping into the darkness of the Brittany countryside at what seemed an alarming rate.

The landing shock, or so the experts inform me, is rather similar to that experienced when jumping from a fourteen foot wall. In my case I made unexpected contact with the roof of a barn and broke a leg, which led to a rather lengthy convalescence in company with an old Breton sea captain turned farmer who showed me some interesting tricks with a knife, which is another story entirely.

On subsequent occasions, I avoided any possible repetition by choosing other modes of entry. It was possible to fly in by Lysander or Hudson and I did this on several occasions. Indeed, on that final operation in the Vosges, I went in with four tons of supplies and ammunition in a DC3 and there was always Spain and the scramble over the Pyrenees.

But salt water being to a certain extent in my blood, a fast boat and a passage by night was the way for me and I'd done it so many times that the routine was almost second nature.

Usually clients were brought down from London to a hotel in Torquay to await the Navy's pleasure, for the C.-in-C. Plymouth had the last word about departure times. Uniform was invariably worn for security reasons.

It was usual to go on board the depot ship of the 15th MGB Flotilla at Falmouth around noon on the great day and one transferred to the operational gunboat five minutes before sailing time and went straight below.

It was strange to be in uniform again, but at least it earned me the commander's cabin for the trip and the kind of deference for rank that you seem to find in the Navy in a way you don't elsewhere.

The commander was a lieutenant of about my own age called Dobson. He had a thin, rather reckless face and wore his cap Mountbatten style. From the looks of him, he'd thoroughly enjoyed his war and wouldn't know what the hell to do with himself when it was over.

'Nice to have you aboard, sir. Have a word with you later if I may. Like to get under way now.'

He disappeared and a few moments later the great diesel engines rumbled into life and we started to move. There was a tap on the door and Fitzgerald came in. I'd seen him briefly the previous evening at the house on the banks of the Helford River just west of Falmouth where I had been taken in the car Henry had sent to pick me up.

Henry himself had been there with a couple of people from the London end together with Fitzgerald and party. They were exactly as I had expected, hard, tough young men, superbly fit, which I certainly wasn't, and surprisingly well-disciplined. They were checking their equipment and canoes in the garage when I was taken to meet them and Fitzgerald certainly seemed to know what he was about.

He showed me everything with an exquisite politeness that was infinitely worse than any more obvious antagonism could have been and the men, I knew, sensed something in the air, something electric between us that wasn't good.

What was it that irritated me so? His voice, his mannerisms? Or could it have been the beautifully tailored battledress—the ribbons above his tunic pocket on the left-hand side? People in my line don't get medals. I had nothing to show for five-and-half black, brutal years, except my face and that civil list pension which Henry had obtained for me. Some strange jealousy, perhaps or a basic feeling of inferiority common to all small men?

There was no answer—probably never would be and I left them to it and departed with Henry, spending the night at a country pub outside Falmouth posing as an officer on leave from London.

I came back to the present abruptly, aware that Fitzger-

ald was speaking. 'A briefing at 21.00 hours. Is that accepta-
ble, sir?'

'I should imagine so.'

He hesitated, as if about to say something then withdrew. But I had other things to think about and lay back
on the bunk, head pillowed in my hands, staring up at the
bulkhead above my head.

The weather forecast was reasonable for the general
area of the Channel. Three to four with rain squalls, but
easing off towards midnight. But there was no moon and
with the tide running there was no more dangerous spot
on the Atlantic seaboard than the waters around St Pierre.

In the bar of the oldest pub in Charlottestown, the
Man o' War near the South Landing, they had the finest
collection of pictures of wrecks I'd seen anywhere and
some of the photos were Victorian.

I drifted into sleep and when I wakened again, it was
seven-thirty. I got up, opened my holdall, took out denim
pants, my old Guernsey, canvas rope-soled boots, a reefer
coat that my father had worn round the Horn under sail
and an old bosun's cap with a broken peak.

I changed quickly and examined myself in the mirror. I
could have landed in uniform like Fitzgerald and company for the plain truth was that with so few civilians left
on the island, there was no hope that I could pass muster
if challenged. But I was superstitious—the black Celtic
blood in me—and believed in some strange way that uniform was bad luck for me, at least when worn in action.

I'd worn it in defeat out of Dunkirk and never again
until that semi-military operation in the Vosges when I
had tasted defeat for the second time. I had not cared for
the experience overmuch. I touched my eye patch briefly,
and remembered the ear ring. I had removed it on Mary's
insistence, as some mark of respect to my sovereign's uniform. I put it back where it belonged now, a small gesture
of defiance to the lesser gods.

I disliked shoulder-holsters which cannot be got rid of
quickly when faced with a search. The hand gun I took
out of the holdall now was a Mauser with the S.S. bulbous
silencer, a weapon much favoured by the Gestapo, one of
whose members had provided it, and excellent for a reasonably quiet execution, though no pistol known to man
can be completely silenced.

I pushed it into the inside breast pocket of my reefer

coat, put my knife in the right pocket, my rubber torch in
the left, and went out.

I met the Chief Petty Officer on his way down the com-
panion-way and Navy to the hilt he didn't turn a hair at
my appearance. He saluted smartly. 'Captain's compli-
ments, sir. He'd take it as a privilege if you'd join him on
the bridge.'

He held open the door at the top of the companionway
and spray kicked me in the face as I stepped out into the
darkness.

There was no moon, but whitecaps gleamed faintly
through the darkness on either side and there was a considerable amount of phosphorescence in our wake.

When I went on to the bridge, Dobson turned to greet
me, his head disembodied in the light from the chart table. 'Good of you to come up, sir. Thought we might have
a look at the charts together. Major Fitzgerald's already
here.'

Fitzgerald moved out of the shadows. He was dressed
for action in waterproof smock and trousers and his face
had been darkened with camouflage cream. He didn't
speak, but accepted a cigarette when I offered him one.

'I understand you're something of an old hand on this
run, sir?' Dobson said.

I nodded. 'Until a year ago. Is Lieutenant-Commander
Ferguson still active?'

'Posted to Alex nine months ago. Working in the Ae-
gean last I heard, doing the same sort of thing in motor-
ised feluccas.'

'Bit of a difference.'

He grinned. 'He's welcome to it. I wouldn't like to part
with this baby.'

I didn't blame him. The MGB was quite a craft. 117
feet long, her armament ranged from a six-pounder down
to a couple of .303 machine guns and catered for most
tastes in between. With three 1,000 h.p. Diesel engines, she
could cruise comfortably at around 20 knots and push
that up to 25 in any crisis.

'How's the E-boat situation?' I asked.

'Oh, they're still pretty active. Mainly in the Golfe de St
Malo area, but we get them generally in the Channel. The
Americans cleared Brest last year, but most of the other
Brittany ports are still in enemy hands though under siege
from the land side.'

'From where do they operate in the Channel Islands?' Fitzgerald asked him.

'Guernsey mostly. St Peter Port, but as I say, you'll get them almost anywhere in the Channel area. Where you least expect them, that's the trouble.'

'They're that good?'

'Bloody good,' Dobson told him feelingly. 'For a start, they've got quite a turn of speed. Thirty-five knots to be precise, which is ten more than we can do and the blokes in charge seem to know what they're doing.' He grinned cheerfully. 'I can think of nicer ways to go on a dark night.'

We discussed the run-in, the major change of plan involving the pick-up and I gave him some useful information about conditions in the area generally. He tapped his fingers on the Pinnacles half-a-mile north-west of the harbour entrance.

'They look like something to steer clear of.'

'The worst reef on the whole of the North Atlantic seaboard. Twenty-seven major wrecks in the last seventy-five years. A death trap.'

'Nasty.' He made a face. 'Especially with this Mill-Race thing running that you were telling me about. We'll have to be damn careful when the tide's turning, I can see that.'

He made some excuse and left us for a while. There was the helmsman of course and a midshipman who seemed to have a pair of night glasses permanently fixed in position. I went outside and stood at the rail, staring into the darkness, thinking about Simone and what lay ahead, but mainly about Simone.

Fitzgerald leaned on the rail beside me. 'We seem to have the sea to ourselves.'

'Very probably. The Navy always cancels its nightly E-boat sweeps when an operation like this is on, I'd have thought you'd have known that.'

Which was unnecessary and I think now that he was trying his damnedest to come to some sort of understanding with me. He changed to the more direct approach. 'You don't like Americans, do you?'

'That's new to me. Admittedly you took your time about coming into the war, but I'd say that showed good sense.'

'All right then,' he said, restraining himself with an effort. 'You don't like me?'

'A reasonable enough deduction.'

'But why?'

'You've got blue eyes,' I said. 'I could never stand blue eyes.' But now I was baiting him and as suddenly, was tired of it. 'Why should it be necessary that I like you?'

But it was, I suppose, because it was something he had always taken for granted back there in that golden New England rich boy's world. I was shaking his foundation, the structure on which he had built his life for he was, as I was to discover, very much the kind of man who believed in the appearance of things, never in the actuality.

He turned to go and I grabbed his arm. 'For heaven's sake, why don't you laugh occasionally. I'll have an American cigarette if you've got one.'

He had and gave it to me. I lit it inside my coat and cupped it in my palm to hide the glowing end. 'Let's put it this way, Major. I don't really like anybody very much. I've spent five-and-a-half years living by my wits over there, fighting the kind of war which hasn't particularly endeared my fellow men to me.'

'You mean the Nazis?'

'I mean everybody. Let me tell you something about war. The side you love to hate comes over to your team next time round. I've worked in the French underground with three distinct and separate organisations who spent as much time trying to do each other down as they did fighting the Germans. It's a game—that's what war is. A dangerous, exciting game that most men thoroughly enjoy playing.'

'If it's a game, then it's a game for heroes,' he said. 'I can't accept it any other way.'

'That sounds like a bad line of dialogue from the kind of Twentieth Century Fox film where the Marines go in to die for democracy, one helmet strap dangling.'

When he answered, he seemed genuinely bewildered. 'I don't get it. The Professor told me all about you. The things you've done over there. He said you were the best there is.'

'The best of what?' I said. 'The rest are either in a concentration camp or dead. Mostly dead.'

'But not you—that's my point. You were over there longer and you survived longer.'

'And you think that evidence of value?' I laughed. 'Let me tell you how I survived. By learning to kill efficiently

and economically as a reflex action, without the slightest
hesitation. Living by that principle has saved my life on a
great many occasions.'

'That sounds okay by me.'

'On the other hand,' I added, 'I killed twice, by mistake,
men who were on our side.' He stared at me through the
darkness, the dim light from the wheel-house reflecting
dully from his eyes. 'I couldn't afford to take a chance,
you understand?'

Spray scattered across us as the MGB bucked a long
wave and Fitzgerald said woodenly. 'I guess you had to do
what you had to do.'

'You're damn right, I did. No trumpets, no standards
flying bravely through the smoke of battle.' I had to smile
at that one. 'Sorry, bad habit of mine that kind of language. I once had pretensions to being a poet.'

He didn't seem to hear me. 'He told me you took on
three thousand crack S.S. fighting troops in the Vosges
with only a couple of hundred guerrillas and held them
for eight days.'

'True enough,' I said. 'Did he remember to tell you we
had women in the mountains as well? At the end of that
little affair, I cowered in a hole in the ground and kept
my mouth shut while eleven S.S. men held one of them
down and took turns. She was still alive when they left.'

'And what did you do?'

'I shot her, Major Fitzgerald. I did what I would have
done for any other dumb animal in agony, broken beyond
any hope of repair.'

He turned and stumbled away, which was not surprising. For him, war *had* been a gallant adventure. Small-
scale raiding across the Channel, action by night. The oc-
casional hand-to-hand encounter, a shot in the dark, the
rattle of a Thompson gun. To his credit, on half-a-dozen
occasions, as I discovered a long time afterwards, he and
his men had successfully penetrated enemy held ports under cover of darkness in their canoes, had placed their
limpet mines and had withdrawn without anyone being
any the wiser.

His contribution to the Normandy landing had been essential, extremely dangerous, but unspectacular. His party
had cleared mines on Omaha three nights before D-Day.
In fact, he had never taken part in a large scale action,
had never seen a country ravaged by the armies that

fought over it, had never seen women and children at risk.
And yet, he was a brave man. Brave, but as I decided
then, a little stupid. I moved back into the wheel-house
and Dobson appeared.

'Turning the silencer on now, sir.'

Which meant that we were approximately thirty miles
from our destination for there was a standard drill on
these occasions. At fifteen miles the main engines would
go completely and we would proceed in silence on the
auxiliaries. At half-a-mile, I would be off-loaded and
taken the rest of the way in a surf boat.

Dobson checked his watch. 'Final briefing just coming
up, sir. I arranged with Major Fitzgerald to use the ward
room. Shall we go down?'

'Grande Pierre is an operation which falls into two direct parts,' I said. 'Task number one is mine. To land and
obtain what intelligence I can. Task number two is yours.
To penetrate the harbour at Charlottestown and mine
whatever craft you discover there.'

They bunched around the table on which the map lay,
their faces, like Fitzgerald's, darkened with camouflage
cream so that it was not possible to get even an inkling of
what was going on in their minds. Not that it mattered.
I'd done this kind of thing so often during the past five
years that consequences no longer figured in my calcula-
tions. The fact that some of these men, or all of them,
could be dead before morning was just another cold hard
fact of war.

They knew exactly what was supposed to happen, every
last detail of the operation. Sufficient reason to go through
it all again which was what I proceeded to do.

When I was finished with technical details, I added a
few remarks for good measure. 'Three final points so that
we all know exactly where we stand. First and foremost,
my mission is more important than yours and *must* repeat
must take precedence at all times.'

There was a nasty gleam in Grant's eye at that one and
I went on, 'Secondly, there is to be no question of any attempt to destroy shore-based installations or in any way to
act in a manner likely to inform the enemy of your
presence.' Fitzgerald had every excuse for annoyance at
the way I'd slipped that one in, but his only expression of
anger was a noticeable tightening of the facial muscles.

'Last of all,' I said, 'if any of this goes wrong, if plans have to be altered in any way, I'm in command.'

That did provoke something of a stir, but Fitzgerald moved in sharply to nip it in the bud. 'All right, back to the mess deck now for a final equipment check.' He turned and said quietly. 'You'd like to inspect them, Colonel?'

I nodded. 'I'll be along in ten minutes.'

He saluted and withdrew. I grinned at Dobson who was frowning slightly. 'Deep waters, eh, Dobson? Never mind. You'll oblige me with a very large whisky and then I'll give those lads the once-over for the last time.'

Strange how remarkably like a colonel I could sound when I wanted to.

It was all very regimental. They stood by their canoes at attention, weighed down with equipment, exactly as they would go in at zero hour. Hard, tough, competent fighting men. Looking at them now, I had to admit that you couldn't ask for much better.

Each man wore a camouflaged waterproof smock and trousers, knitted Commando cap and carried a Thompson sub-machine gun, grenades, Commando knife, and various bits of miscellaneous equipment about the person including a repair kit in event of damage to the canoes, which proved that somebody had a macabre sense of humor in the section concerned with amphibious warfare. The limpet mines were carried in carefully partitioned canvas bags, one to a canoe.

I said to Fitzgerald. 'I'm glad they're on my side, Major.'

He was pleased and tried not to show it. 'Thank you, sir.'

'They're familiar with the provisions of the Kommandobefehl?'

'Perfectly.'

'Fair enough.' I turned to the men. 'Just so you realise it's odds on to a bullet in the back of the head if they get their hands on you.'

I walked out followed by Dobson. 'A tough bunch of men,' he observed. 'I took a group of Rangers in before D-Day to clear some of the beach approaches. Never seen anything like it for sheer bloody nerve.'

'Men like that have only one fault,' I said as we went

up on deck. 'They never know when to give up which means they usually go too far. That can sometimes be disastrous.'

Strange that I should say that. Out of some weird foreknowledge, I suppose. The kind of thing the scientist tells us isn't possible. And yet I knew in my bones that something was going to go wrong. *The Celt in me again.* Knew it as certainly as if it had already happened as I stood on the bridge staring into the darkness.

It was some little time later that Dobson and Fitzgerald found me. 'Tea, sir?' Dobson passed me an enamel mug. 'Well laced with the usual.'

God bless the Navy. The rum exploded into a warm and wonderful glow. The rain was rather heavier now and Dobson took a deep breath. 'This is what I like. This is about everything there is.'

'What were you doing before the war?'

'Accountant's office.'

I felt a sudden sympathy for him. 'Will you go back?'

'In a pig's eye!' he said forcibly. 'I'll sign on a Panamanian before the mast first.' He laughed lightly. 'Anyway, I haven't survived the war yet, have I, sir?'

Fitzgerald said, 'I shouldn't have thought there was much doubt of that at this stage.'

'Men generally die in war when they cannot help it and are defeated by a disadvantageous situation,' I quoted. Fitzgerald turned to look at me, his face a blur in the darkness and I added helpfully. *'The Art of War* by a Chinese soldier called Wu Ch'i, Major. I commend it to you. He said everything there is to be said on the subject back in 400 BC.'

'I'm sorry, but I can't accept that.' he told me politely. 'A soldier dies not by circumstances alone, but out of his own inability to meet the challenge of the particular situation.'

Which had probably looked good on the blackboard at West Point or wherever it was he had received officer training. I could have given him some more Wu Ch'i but there didn't seem to be much point.

When we stopped, there was nothing to be seen of the island which was as it should be and when they put the surf boat over, I was feeling surprisingly cheerful thanks to that final mug of tea and Dobson's generous helping of navy rum.

I was being taken in by the midshipman who was called
Varley and a tough old seaman named Dawson. They
went over the side and waited for me and Dobson
checked his watch.

'Right, sir, off you go then and the best of British . . .'

He shook hands and saluted formally and Fitzgerald
loomed out of the darkness. 'Good luck, Colonel.'

He was formal enough about it, but his handshake was
firm. I was still far from happy. There was something
badly wrong and it was to do with this man or perhaps it
would be fairer to say the both of us. It had been a bad
relationship from the beginning. He had started it off on
the wrong foot and I had reacted accordingly and that
had been very much that. Still, there was nothing to be
done about it now and I went over the side and dropped
into the boat.

Landings by night on the enemy coast have always been
something of a problem. Good beaches tended to be
mined. The other kind were usually dangerous for more
obvious reasons. Surf boats had been designed to minimise
the hazards and in the hands of trained personnel, were
reliable in most conditions. On top of that, they were
treated with a special kind of paint that made them almost
impossible to detect from even quite short distances.

I could hear the surf through the darkness before I
could see the island, the waves crashing against the cliffs
and then, quite suddenly, as if a veil had been lifted, I
could see phosphorescence and clouds of white spray shining through the darkness.

I checked the compass again, and tapped Varley on the
shoulder. 'Straight in and then I'll see what I can remember.'

The current had us now, water slapping against the hull
and there were rocks standing jaggedly above white water.
We slipped in among them like a wraith and drifted no
more than a couple of yards from the cliff face.

From there, I had to play it by ear. It had been a long
time, a hell of a long time and yet there are things one
can never forget, things that are a part of one as surely as
life itself.

I could hear a strange, hollow groaning, the distinctive
voice of the bore hole that lay at the bottom of the Devil's

Staircase and tapped Varley on the shoulder again, giving him directions.

There was room for us to drift inside, but only by bending our heads. Varley and Dawson steadied the surf boat and I switched on my torch and stood up. Salt water, seaweed and slime—the air was full of it and the stench of old bird droppings. The ledge I sought was a couple of feet above my head. Varley held the torch for me and I pulled myself up.

He handed me the torch and then a one-man inflatable dinghy, neatly packaged, supposedly a kind of insurance if anything went wrong with the surf boat.

He smiled. 'Best of luck, sir. We'll be back dead on time, I promise you.'

A slight scraping sound, a splash from the oars and they were gone and I was alone and yet not alone. Home again for the first time in five long years.

5   On Dangerous Ground

I found a suitable crevasse well above high water mark, pushed the inflatable dinghy inside and then took stock of the situation. The jagged shaft vanished into total darkness above me, slanting to the right. About fifty feet above my head, it changed direction, inclining sharply towards the left. And so it continued, zig-zagging upwards three hundred feet to an exit hole in a crevasse in the rock just below the cliff top.

I had climbed it first as a boy of fourteen as part of a kind of island ritual that was supposed to prove whether you had guts or not. It had been a memorable experience. I had followed the same route on two further occasions. Once to impress Simone, the reason for so many things in those days, and on the final attempt, to prove something to myself.

The difference now was that for a great deal of the time I must climb in darkness, but there was no possible alternative. I flashed the torch upwards, tried to memorise what lay ahead, then put it in my pocket and started to climb.

The plain truth is that in a way it was something of an anti-climax. There was plenty of hand and foot holds and perhaps the all-embracing darkness that prevented me from seeing what lay below was a help rather than a hindrance.

I climbed steadily with hardly a pause for ten or fifteen minutes and the hollow booming of the sea faded and I was quite alone. For most of the way, it seemed so easy that I couldn't quite accept the reality of it, remembering that boy with his young heart in his mouth. There were two possible explanations, I suppose. That it had never been as difficult as I had remembered or that I was a damned sight more competent at doing this kind of thing now than I was then.

The final fifty or sixty feet were the worst by far, for at that point the shaft became vertical, and in places it was only possible to progress by wedging between the sides and moving a foot at a time.

I could smell the cold air again now and rain drifted down in a fine spray and when I glanced up, there was a lighter patch in the darkness and a glint of a star. I paused for a breath then inched my way up the last fifteen or twenty feet without stopping. A moment later, my hands had a grip on the rim of the exit hole and I hauled myself out.

I crouched on a small ledge and took in several lungfuls of good fresh air. There was a feeling of enormous space, of a void out there in the darkness into which one might pitch headforemost and fall for ever. Three hundred feet below the surf was a smear of white and above, the stars glittered through holes in the clouds.

Now that I was on dangerous ground where anything could happen, I took the Mauser from my pocket and secured it to the spring clip at the rear of my belt, then I started to make my way up a gently sloping fissure of rock to the cliff top. I paused on the edge, my hands digging into wet turf, the smell of it filling my nostrils with a strange, nostalgic pleasure. Smells, after all, can be more evocative than almost anything else.

I got to my feet, peering into the darkness, took a first step forward and tripped headlong over a strand of barbed wire and alarm canisters started to rattle on either side of me.

The first conscious thought was that Joe St Martin had

betrayed me. Either that, or the wire defence system at that point had been erected within the past three weeks which didn't seem possible. Remembering his final words, it seemed more than likely now that he had sent me deliberately to my death.

My heavy reefer coat had saved me from being shredded on the barbs, but for the moment, I was securely hooked. As I started to free myself, section-by-section, a door banged, there was a brief flash of light and then it closed.

The voices, when they sounded, were German. My cup couldn't have been fuller. 'Who goes there? Stand and declare yourself.'

I pulled myself free, the alarm canisters rattling again as I slid backwards towards the edge of the cliff, but I was too late. A torch beam picked me out of the darkness and I got my hands up fast before it could be followed by a burst from a machine pistol.

'No—for pity's sake, don't shoot! I'm only a fisherman! A simple fisherman, that's all!'

I managed to inject a certain amount of terror into my voice which wasn't all that difficult and gave it to them in French with a strong Breton accent.

The torch beam stayed on my face and the reply came in words instead of bullets. In halting French I was asked to explain myself. I said that I was a fisherman from Prente du Chateaux on the Brittany coast. The engine of my boat had broken down, I had drifted helplessly for six hours and had finally come to grief on the rocks at the bottom of the cliffs.

It must have seemed convincing enough and I was certainly dressed for the part. They discussed the situation together in German and from the sound of it, they were simply ordinary soldiers on guard duty. What seemed to intrigue them the most was the fact that I had somehow managed to climb the cliffs which I must have done for I was there, wasn't I, on the other side of the wire?

I started to lower my hands and was sharply reminded to keep them raised. The torch beam never left my face for a moment. I could hear a metallic rustling as a section of the wire was rolled back, a solid curse or two in good Saxon German as someone pricked himself. A moment later, he was beside me.

I could have taken him there and then in several different ways, but that still left the man on the other side of the wire, so I submitted patiently to the clumsy and inexpert search.

He found nothing for my knife was concealed in the palm of my right hand which was raised with its fellow obediently over my head and even an expert might have missed the Mauser on its clip at the small of my back. He wasn't, after all, expecting to find anything—anything important, that is.

He took out the torch, pressed the button and indicated the path through the wire. I went obediently. I didn't get much of a look at his friend in passing. I was still partially blinded from the glare of the torch, but I got the impression that he was in charge.

'No, Karl, put the wire back later. Let's have a look at him inside first.'

We walked no more than ten yards and went down steps to a concrete observation post of a type to be found in their thousands all along the Atlantic seaboard. That settled it. St Martin must have known. *Had to know.* This thing had obviously been built for several years.

'Open the door!' I was ordered in that same halting French.

I did as I was told and went down three steps into the lighted bunker. There was no one else there, could not be for there was no other door. I turned and faced my captors.

The one in front was middle-aged with grey hair and steel glasses—an Artilleryman from his uniform. The one behind him looked a different calibre altogether with hard, bitter eyes and an old bullet scar on the side of the face. He hung his machine pistol on a peg near the door and took out a cigarette, looking me over curiously.

The man with the steel spectacles held my torch in one hand and a rifle in the other. He poked me with the barrel and grinned. 'Hands high. Come on—get them up!'

A fair proportion of the time allotted to the training course run for agents of S.O.E. and similar organisations, was devoted to the art of silent killing, the chief instructor being a man of terrifying efficiency in his field. At the end of his course, any fear of a physical hand-to-hand encounter I might ever have held—which after all, can only be a fear of being beaten or injured—had so far left me that I never again felt the slightest fear about taking on anybody and I was smaller than the average. In fact one's greatest fear at the end of the course was the possibility of ever being involved in a brawl in which one might kill the other man as a reflex action.

I have walked out of more bars for this reason when things started looking ugly, taken insults from drunks on the London tube more than once, although strangely enough, the feeling of complete power and self-confidence makes it relatively simple to walk away.

Be that as it may, there had never been the slightest doubt in my mind that I would kill the two sentries on the cliff top that night. Would have to kill them.

The man in the steel spectacles smiled and prodded me again. I started to raise my hands, sprung the blade of the gutting knife, an old Commando trick this, and stabbed him under the chin, the blade shearing up through the roof of the mouth into the brain, killing him instantly. He lurched to one side, pulling the knife from my grasp and the other man grabbed for his machine pistol with a curse. The Mauser with the S.S. bulbous silencer was already in my left hand and I shot him though the heart at almost point blank range.

It was about ten seconds later that the field telephone rang. To have allowed it to go unanswered would have been fatal or so it seemed then, but I was in another world now. A private world where action follows thought on the instant and the thinking seems clearer, the senses sharper, than ever before.

I lifted the phone, muffled the speaker slightly with one hand and said in German. 'Hello.'

A voice crackled faintly along a bad line. 'Muller, that you? Weber here. Everything in order?'

'Everything fine,' I said.

'Good. See you in the morning.'

I replaced the phone and got to work. I retrieved my knife, cleaned it and put it away together with the torch, then I turned my attention to the bodies on the floor. Neither of them had bled very much. I took the one with steel spectacles first, hoisted him over my shoulders, went outside, and threw him over the cliffs. Then I returned for his friend.

I replaced the wire, masking the way through, went back into the bunker and checked the floor. There was a small amount of blood and I got a damp cloth from the lavatory and swabbed it up. From the sound of that phone call there was an excellent chance that the post would not be visited until morning, but one could never be certain of anything in this life. If anyone did call unexpectedly, they might think the guards were on patrol. If they found blood, the whole island would be seething within fifteen minutes.

There was a bicycle in the porch outside and it gave me an idea. Time was the thing now and every minute saved might count for a great deal in the long run. The sentries' greatcoats hung behind the door. I took one, stuffed my bosun's cap into its pocket and tried on a steel helmet that lay on the table. It was a couple of sizes too large for me which was all to the good and I left quickly, got the bicycle and wheeled it along the track.

My mind was working faster than ever now, considering what to do. The path I was on would bring me, after a quarter of a mile, to a dirt road, originally built to serve Fort Marie Louise in Victorian times. That road would lead me to Charlottestown or Granville and the Seigneurie was on the Granville section. It seemed logical that a German soldier on his bicycle could get there a damned sight faster than Owen Morgan on foot, blundering across fields that might hold more surprises than Joe St Martin had ever indicated.

A few moments later, the feel of the track beneath my feet seemed to change and when I switched on the hooded bicycle lamp, I discovered why. It had been surfaced with tarmacadam. Indeed, as I was to discover later, the Germans had metalled most of the old dirt roads and tracks on the island for reasons of efficiency during the period when they were constructing the mass of their fortifications.

It certainly made things easier for me and I mounted the bicycle and rode away.

It was a little over a mile to the Seigneurie and for most of the way I didn't come across a soul. As I neared the airstrip and prepared to turn left into Granville road, I saw hooded headlights approaching. It was too late to get out of sight so I slowed, keeping my head down and gave way. A truck turned past me into the Granville road. I had an impression that the driver waved and then it disappeared into the night.

I went down the hill, my stomach hollow. A few hundred yards—that was all—a few hundred yards to Simone. What would she say? How would she react? Would she recognise me even? No, that wasn't likely at all.

I came round a corner and found the Seigneurie below in the hollow among the beech trees and there were lights in the courtyard, dim, certainly, but allowing enough illuminations for me to see that something was very wrong indeed. There were at least three field cars down there and a limousine and there was a sentry at the bottom of the steps leading up to the porched entrance, the Nazi flag hanging from a pole above him.

Joe St Martin again. There would have to be a reckoning there. Very much so. I cycled past the front gate where the truck I had previously seen was just turning in and kept on going.

Granville lay below me in the darkness, a hamlet of no more than a dozen or fifteen cottages clustered around the old lifeboat station. Granville where—according to Joe St Martin—Ezra Scully lived on alone. Had he lied about that also? But that I had to find out for myself—had no other choice. I went down through the darkness till I came to the first house, dismounted and left the bicycle behind a hedge.

There was an unearthly stillness to everything. It was a village of the dead. Nothing lived here and somewhere in the distance the sea cried softly.

I moved on cautiously. Ezra's cottage was behind the lifeboat shed. I could see no reason for him to have changed unless under duress. And then I paused, for I could see a chink of light at one of his windows, hear muffled laughter.

I crouched at the windows by his front door and peered through a crack between the curtains. He sat on the far side of the table in his shirt sleeves, positioned so that I could look him full in the face and he had hardly changed. The same craggy, used up face, the same great red beard, his bald crown shining in the light from the naked bulb above his head. Electricity in Granvill now? Presumably another German innovation.

He had three companions—German soldiers, also in shirt sleeves. There was a crate of beer on the floor and they were playing whist if I knew my Ezra. I stood up and moved away. I could have taken all three of them as they sat there, but that was not the way to handle it with Ezra there. A moment later there was a roar of laughter, a chair scraped and someone opened the door.

It was one of the Germans. I moved into the shadows and found myself against the rear wall of the boathouse. There was a door at my back. When I tested the latch, it opened at my touch and I moved quietly into the darkness and closed it again. The cottage door closed, cutting off the voices. I waited for a moment then took out my torch.

And I couldn't believe what I saw when I flashed it briefly. In the darkness I moved closer and ran my hand along her counter and she spoke to me, every lovely familiar inch of her. She was a 41-foot Watson-type motor life-boat. Twin-screw, weighed fifteen tons and was powered by two 35 h.p. petrol engines. She carried a crew of eight and in rough weather could take fifty people on board.

For a moment the years slipped away and I could see the great twenty-foot curtains of green water rolling in to crush us, felt myself go and fell into the rear cockpit to fetch up against the legs of the man at the wheel. He cried out, his voice drowned in the roaring of the wind, eye flaring beneath the yellow sou'wester, salt water streaming through his beard. Ezra Scully, coxswain of the St Pierre life-boat, one of the greatest names in the history of the life-boat service.

He kicked me in the ribs, driving me to my feet and I grabbed for a safety line. I was nineteen, home on vacation at the end of my first year at University and there was nowhere on earth I would have wanted to be other than that boat at that precise moment in time.

As I reached my feet, we poised on the crest of an enormous wave and beyond, through the rain, I saw the cargo boat we were after rolling helplessly from side to side.

I ran a hand across my eyes to clear away salt water and found myself again in the quiet darkness, alone with a 41-foot Watson-type motor life-boat named the *Owen Morgan*.

Not all lifeboatmen are fishermen. In Northumberland you'll find miners in the crews. In Wales, farmers. It would be dangerous for me to claim that my father was the only artist to serve as a second coxswain, but it seems likely. On the other hand, he had been bred to the sea and for many years had earned his living by it, so perhaps the distinction is invidious.

The boat which killed him was named *Ceciley Jackson*, and was a 35-footer. Small as life-boats go, she had been built for beach launching and had to be light. The main harbour on St Pierre was unsuitable for use as a life-boat station, because there were many occasions of tide and weather when it would have been impossible for the boat to get out of the harbour.

The *Ceciley Jackson* was of the self-righting type and if capsized was supposed to come up again, even with a hole in her bottom although this could not be guaranteed.

I was fourteen when it happened in the spring of 1932. A Norwegian coaster had gone aground on the Pinnacles in the early hours and the *Ceciley Jackson* had been launched just before dawn.

There wasn't a soul on the island who wasn't on the ramparts of Fort Edward that morning. The Pinnacles were just over half a mile out, one of the greatest hazards to shipping in the area and the weather was worsening by the minute. I can still recall the strangely matter-of-fact wording of the Royal Lifeboat Institution's report on the affair, for there are heroes ten-a-penny in their files.

. . . In the early hours of 2nd April, 1932 the Norwegian steamer *Viking* went aground on the Pinnacles three miles N.W. of the harbour of Charlottes-town on St Pierre in the Channel Islands. The vessel's radio was out of action and distress flares were observed on shore at 5.00 a.m. Owing to the severity of the weather it was an hour before the life-boat *Ceciley Jackson* a 35-foot, self-righting type, could be launched with the assistance of every available able-

bodied man. A wind speed of over 90 knots was recorded by the harbourmaster about that time and the
seas were described by onlookers as mountainous. At
7.30 a.m. Coxswain Ezra Scully took. . .

Six closely typed pages. I could have gone on, for every
word was branded on my brain, but it could be more simply told. The *Viking* was grinding herself to death on the
most dangerous reef in the Channel Islands in near-hurri-
cane conditions and only a miracle worker could hope to
get close enough to give the eighteen men on board a
chance to jump. In that place of cross currents and whirl-
pool, there was no hope of firing a line to her for it would
have parted in seconds.

But the *Ceciley Jackson* had her genius—Ezra Scully—
and he took the boat in with a rush, no more than a foot
in it for five vital seconds, playing his engines to hold him
there, nailed into place as two jumped for their lives. Again
he repeated the performance and yet again, smashing his
bows badly at one point as a cross current caught him.

And at last there was only one man left, one terrified
human being clinging half-way down the ladder. On the
last run-in, my father reached for him and the poor
wretch would not let go. Neither would my father, for he
was that kind of man and as the *Cecily Jackson* sheered
off, he went over, still hanging on to the sailor and they
both went into the sea. Already the tide was running, the
dreaded Coursier, the Mill Race of St Pierre. It caught the
life-boat, sending her back against the *Viking*, once, twice,
three times, crushing the life out of Owen Morgan.

And on the run back to Charlottestown, tragedy struck
again. The *Ceciley Jackson*'s bows were already badly
damaged and three of her six watertight compartments
were taking water. She made it into harbour and then a
tremendous wave roared in from the Channel, turned her
over, righted again and splintered her against the granite
walls of the old Admiralty breakwater.

Eight more had died that cold morning, but the rest, including Ezra Scully, had been saved, dragged from the
surf and boiling waters by the human chain that snaked
across the rocks.

So my father died and my mother with him although
she walked the earth for another seven years.

And Ezra received a bar to his gold medal from the National Lifeboat Institution and funds were raised by public subscription to build a boat-house and concrete slipway at the bottom of the hill at Granville and a new life-boat to go with it. A 41-foot, Watson-type named the *Owen Morgan.*

My memories of that fatal morning were so intense, so painful, that for a little while they drove out all thought of my present situation. It was the click of the latch that brought me back to reality.

I had heard no footfall, caught as I was by old memories and already the door was opening. There was no time to run but as it closed and the light was switched on, I had the Mauser ready in my hand. Ezra stared at me stupidly, half-drunk, a crate of empty beer bottles swinging from one hand.

He'd certainly picked up a very fair knowledge of German since we'd last met. 'Who are you?' he demanded. 'What are you doing here?'

I took off the steel helmet. 'Hello, Uncle Ezra,' I said softly, which was the way in which I had addressed him as a boy although our blood relationship was limited, he being my mother's cousin twice removed.

But he had been like a father to me after the death of my own, had loved me almost as much as he had loved my mother and she, I believe, had been the one great passion of his life.

His voice dropped to a whisper and he placed the crate down on the floor. 'Owen?' he said. 'Is that you, lad?'

'As ever was, Ezra.'

He came close, reached up and touched my face gently, a kind of wonder on his own. 'By God, lad, what have they done to you?'

'The war, Ezra—the war.'

He nodded slowly, gripped me in a brief, embarrassed bear-hug, then pushed me away, glaring fiercely, his eyes moist. 'What's this then? What's the bloody game? Different from last time you came, Owen, back in nineteen forty.'

'You know about that?'

'The following day—Simone told me.' He shook his head. 'Owen Morgan's son a soldier—the disgrace of it.

What was wrong with the Navy?'

'A combination of circumstances, Ezra. I'll tell you about it one day. Where's Simone?'

'Lives in the cottage at La Falaise now on her own. The Jerries use the Seigneurie as a field hospital. Old Riley runs it for them.'

The final nail into Joe St Martin's coffin. But I'd no time for him now, even in thought. 'Now listen carefully, Ezra,' I said. 'I haven't got much time. What do you know about the Nigger installation?'

'So that's why you're here? How did you know about that?'

I told him about St Martin. 'A pity,' he said, filling his pipe from an old leather pouch, 'I'd hoped the bastard was herring bait by now, you're wasting your time, Owen. Nothing for you here. The whole Nigger project's flat on its face. Lack of torpedoes, see? On top of that, most of the lads concerned have been killed. Brittany U-boat bases that are still in German hands are heavily blockaded. Difficult for supply boats to get through.'

'You seem remarkably well informed.'

'We listen to the B.B.C. news every night,' he said. 'One of the sergeants billeted on me has a radio.' He hesitated. 'No trouble there, Owen, for my sake. They're good lads, all of them. Good friends of mine. Pioneers, mostly.'

'Fair enough,' I said. 'As long as we don't meet headon.'

'You don't hate them, then?'

'Germans?' I shook my head. 'I've come across a few ripe specimens over the past five years I didn't have much time for, French, German and English. People are still people, good, bad, indifferent.'

He nodded slowly. 'So that we understand each other. I'd take it hard if any of those lads out there came to harm from you, Owen.' He shook his head. 'I don't know what you've been through, lad, but you look capable of most things. What did they make of you?'

'Hard to put into words, Ezra,' I said, 'I'm a colonel now, if that's any use to you.'

His eyes widened. 'Young for that, aren't you? Only two explanations. Either they're hard-pressed over there which don't seem likely now, or you're bloody good at your work. What happens now?'

'I'd like to see Simone if I can, then I'll be leaving. Not

for long now though. On its last legs this war.' I tapped the hull of the *Owen Morgan*. 'Got the shock of my life when I found this old beauty in here. Don't tell me she's still in use.'

He chuckled. 'She ain't been out of the shed since July 1940, when Jerry came, but she's in apple-pie trim. Engine sweet as a nut. I check her every week, see? If it were daylight you'd see where a stray bomb landed on the slipway during the original invasion. Never been able to get her out. A German Navy officer turned up five years ago to inspect her with a view of taking her away, but he decided it were more trouble than it were worth. The beach is mined even if she could be hauled down there, so they've let her be.'

I said slowly. 'One more thing, Ezra. Do you know Steiner?'

'Manfred Steiner?' He nodded slowly. 'Course I do. Everyone knows Manfred.' He frowned. 'Just a minute now. How would you . . .'

'Joe St Martin,' I said. 'He tells me Steiner's the important man where the Nigger installation is concerned. What's he like?'

'Well now.' He frowned. 'That's a hard question to answer. To tell you the truth, lad, he's not like any other man I ever knew. He's a Brandenberger—they're a special breed of men as far as I can see. He's got all the medals any man could ever want and he paints like an angel. Almost as good as your dear father and could I say fairer than that?'

'St Martin seemed to get the impression he was friendly with Simone.'

He knew what was in my mind and made no attempt to deny it, his face grave. 'Friends and more than friends, Owen, I'd say. It's been a long war, lad, and she a young woman in her prime. Would you expect her to wither on the branch?'

He was right as always, and I took some kind of comfort from it. 'All right, Ezra, point taken.'

The cottage door opened, a door banged. 'Ezra? What's keeping you? Where's that beer?'

'Better go.' He pulled a crate from beneath an old work bench. 'Can't have them coming in here. I don't trust you, Owen. You've changed, lad.'

'One thing, Ezra,' I said hurriedly. 'Don't board anything that floats in the harbour in the morning. It won't be for long.'

His face went grey and he said with some bitterness. 'Like that, is it, Owen?' So I let my friends die, do I?'

He switched off the light and left, banging the door behind him, leaving me alone in the darkness, aware that there were times when I had really had enough of the whole sorry business.

I retrieved the bicycle and went back the way I had come. La Falaise was the name of a small valley a quarter of a mile from the cliffs at the south-west corner of the island and not very far from my landing point. A retired Indian Army officer had rented it before the war, but he had been evacuated with those of the islanders who had expressed a desire to leave just before the German occupation. I had met him, quite by chance, in St James's Park in the summer of 1943 and we had retired to the nearest bar for something of a reunion.

It was south from where the road turned to Fort Marie Louise and was the only dwelling in the area close to what was left of a Bronze Age village. The way down to it had never been more than a sunken cart track and it was still so.

The cottage was rather more substantial than the name implied. Originally built in Georgian times, it had been added to in the middle of the nineteenth century during the days of the island's greatest population when the forts were being constructed. I remembered it most for the magnificent views it gave over the sea towards the Brittany coast.

I pushed the bike behind the nearest hedge, stripped off the overcoat and helmet, covered them with brushwood and went forward cautiously.

I came to the entrance to the courtyard at the rear of the cottage and paused. A vehicle was parked there. I moved closer and found that it was a VW field car.

A dog barked hollowly five or six fields away, Alsatian from the sound of it. I thought about that for a while, then moved round to the front of the cottage.

Light showed faintly at the bottom of the curtain of the first window, but I could not see inside. I moved past the front porch and tried the next window. It was something of a shock to find him so close to me. Steiner, I mean, for it had to be him. He sat on the other side of the room at an easel and painted with water colours, my father's favourite medium. He was in his shirt sleeves, uniform trousers and boots and in spite of his intense concentration, there was a slight, good-humoured quirk to his mouth, the sardonic look of a man who had seen the worst life has to offer and who refused to take it seriously.

He had dark, curling hair that was prematurely white at the temples, another little mememto of the Russian campaign as I was to discover later, and a strong, bony face that was full of character. Soldier, scholar—he could have been either. Circumstances would decide with a man like that. Had decided. I could not see what he was painting, could see nothing to the left of me where he occasionally glanced, so I moved to the window at the other end of the cottage to see if I could do any better. The curtain gaped wider than ever there, a band of yellow light cutting through the darkness, I dropped to one knee and peered inside. My hands tightened on the window ledge.

Simone de Beaumarchais posed at the far end of the room, a length of blue silk around her waist, a touch of arrogance in the way she stood there, breasts naked, one hand on hip. It seemed that she was looking towards me, but that wasn't possible. It was Steiner she looked at, Steiner for whom she smiled, so that the heart turned over in me. Had she ever smiled at me like that? Had she ever . . . ? And suddenly, I could taste salt on my lips, taste salt on her flesh, my back warm in the sun, and the earth moved.

The great ever-present hazard in the St Pierre area, even in good weather, is the thick sea-fog that appears from nowhere, reducing visibility to a few yards and it can make small boat sailing very dangerous. In 1935 on the day following Simone's nineteenth birthday, a day of high summer, we took to sea in a new ten-foot sailing dinghy, a present from her father.

It was a day of heat and cloudless sky and the island was a painted backcloth. I should have been warned, but she was like a child with a new toy and wanted to sail to the Pinnacles and for me, she could do no wrong, not then or ever.

Three miles out, she tangled a line and fouled the sail and in the panic which followed, we turned over. There was no hope of righting the dinghy. I tried and failed and finally got Simone up across the keel and hung on beside her, hoping for the best, hoping most of all that the dinghy would continue to float although we were both wearing life-jackets. And then the island disappeared and fog rolled in and perhaps half an hour later, the dinghy decided to go down like a stone.

Until that moment we had managed to make it seem funny for in the heat of that summer afternoon, the water was warm enough, for a time at any rate. But the tide was beginning to turn now, Le Coursier, the Mill-Race, rippling the water all around us, running like a river in spate, a ten-knot current carrying us along in its implacable grip.

And it was the Mill-Race that saved us, that was the strange thing—that and the life-jackets. We were three miles from Charlottestown, close to the Pinnacles and the current skirted the northern coast and turned, brushing against the south-east corner of St Pierre before moving on towards Brittany.

I unbuckled my belt and lashed us together and for an hour-and-a-half, we floated, carried relentlessly through the curtain of grey and then, with startling suddenness there was the thunder of surf, white water crashing in across great, black rocks.

A cliff looked out of the greyness on my left, white with bird lime and gulls called harshly to each other, a storm petrel came in across the water followed by half a dozen more and then the waves took us in together in a great crashing maelstrom of white water and deposited us on the sloping sands of La Grande Bay.

I remember getting an arm round her and staggering forward as another wave crashed in and then we were safe and she was lying on her face, coughing up water.

I got rid of my life-jacket and wet shirt and turned her over. It was no later than three in the afternoon and the sun through the fog was like a furnace and yet she shivered violently for she had been too long out there.

I untied her life-jacket. She wore shorts and an old Guernsey sweater of her father's at least three sizes too big and it was heavy with water. I pulled it over her head and her limbs were like rubber, no resistance there at all.

I got what else she was wearing off her as best I could and started to massage her cold limbs. She was still shaking and after a while I took her in my arms and held her close. I can remember kissing her forehead, her naked breasts crushed against me, telling her over and over again that it was all right now. That it was over.

What happened next was, I suppose, rather obvious and completely natural. I can remember her kissing me, her hand behind my head, the salt taste of her lips, of her skin, the sun warm on my back.

'Love me, Owen, love me.'

I did then, always had, always would. Flesh of my flesh? No, more than that. Part of *me* and everything that meant.

She pulled on an old dressing gown, Steiner was buttoning his tunic. Medals are a hobby of mine, part of my stock in trade. They tell you a great deal about people. Where they've come from, which is always interesting, the deeds they've performed or pretended to perform.

The Germans wore their wound badges on the breast like the star of an order. Steiner's was the silver which meant he'd been wounded three or four times. I wasn't surprised, particularly when I saw his ribbon for the Eastern front campaign of 1941-2. Besides the Iron Cross 2nd class and various other more usual bits and pieces, he had the Iron Cross 1st class, which they weren't in the habit of giving away. He and Fitzgerald had a lot in common. He had a scarf knotted carelessly about his neck. It was some time before I discovered it concealed the Knight's Cross which, as I found later, he'd earned for his exploits with the Danube Group.

They moved towards the door, I stood in the shadows and watched. The door opened, there was a light, gay laugh, 'Tomorrow, nice and early. We'll go for a ride—all right?'

His English was perfect, but her voice was what I wanted to hear. When it came, it was just the same. Strange how there are some things in life we can never forget.

'Tomorrow, then, I'll look forward to it.'

I peered round the corner as he leaned down to kiss her. I was conscious of no emotion at all. No jealousy, no anger, which didn't make sense and yet my mouth was dry and my heart thumped wildly.

She walked a couple of yards with him and he kissed her again and went round the courtyard on his own, singing as he went a strange, melancholy marching song, well known to every man who served on the Russian front in that terrible winter of 1942. *What are we doing here? What is it all about? Alles est veruckt. Everything's crazy. Everything's gone to hell.*

I slipped into the cottage behind her back. The kitchen door stood ajar and I moved inside quickly and waited. The engine of the VW roared into life, the sound moved away along the track, faded into the night. I heard footsteps, the click of the latch. I took a deep breath and stepped into the room.

She stood at the fireplace combing her hair, in the mirror above the mantel and she saw me at once. And then the most amazing thing happened.

'Owen?' she said, 'Owen?'

She had recognized me instantly, black patch, scarred face, five years of hard usage and all, turned and came straight into my arms.

7 Alles est Veruckt

She fed me in the kitchen. There was bread of a sort, flour being in very short supply, home-cured bacon and beer to wash it down. I drank a little and grinned. 'So Ezra's still brewing in his spare time?'

'Not much choice these days. You recognised it?'

'Once tasted, never forgotten.'

She was sitting on the other side of the scrubbed kitchen table and reached across, covering my right hand with her own. 'So long, Owen. So very long.'

'For me, too.' I raised her hand to my mouth, kissed it gently, then held it for a moment against my cheek. There were tears in her eyes. 'Oh, Owen, your poor face. What have they done to you?'

'The first thing Ezra asked.'

'You've seen him?'

'For a short while. I went looking for you at the Seigneurie.' I explained about Joe St Martin and by the time I had finished her face was stiff and angry.

'He always was a loathsome object. I could tell you things, Owen. Things he's done here during the Occupation.'

'Such as?'

'Informing on people who broke regulations. For example, at the beginning of the Occupation, the Germans insisted that all radios were handed in. Many people kept them so that they could listen to the B.B.C. Ezra's had one right through the war. For anyone who was caught, the penalty was severe. A heavy prison sentence served in some labour camp on the Continent. At least half-a-dozen islanders earned that fate because of Joe St Martin.'

'He was an informer?'

She nodded. 'And worse, though it would be difficult to prove more than that.'

We got up and went back into the living room and she put another log on the fire. I got out my cigarettes and gave her one.

She inhaled deeply and sighed. 'I'd forgotten what a Player's tasted like.'

'They're almost as unobtainable on the other side of the Channel.' I lit one myself. 'How bad has it been?'

She shrugged. 'For most of the time, very much as it always was. The past year hasn't been too good. Food shortages and so on. We haven't had a supply boat in for a month.'

'And how have you been treated?'

'On the whole, very fairly. Again, it hasn't been as good during the past year. We got a new governor, a General Muller, just before my father's death. I never liked him. He was S.S. and the staff he brought with him were all S.S. men. I've never liked any of them.'

'Yet this Muller let you stay when almost everyone else was moved out three months back?'

'But I am Seigneur now, Owen. They have to have someone to deal with legally. They're surprisingly formal about such things. And I'm useful you see. Remember my three years at medical school? I help Paddy in the hospital. They really need us.'

'So you don't hate them particularly?'

'It was the Royal Navy who killed my father in its bombardment last year. Should I hate the British for that? And what about you, Owen? You've lost an eye. In action, I suppose?'

'Of a sort.'

'Do you hate them? Is it sufficient cause?'

'The second time I've been asked that tonight.' I shook

my head. 'No, I don't hate them. At the moment they're the other side in the game we're playing which means we do our best to dispose of each other depending on the circumstances. I had trouble with a couple of sentries tonight on the cliffs above the Devil's Staircase where I landed.'

There was a slight frown on her face. 'What happened?'

'They tried to take me prisoner. What do you think happened?'

'You killed? Killed them both?' There was genuine horror on her face. It was only later when I came to realise her position, that I could understand it. For her, these were people she had met every day for years. It was quite possible that the two sentries I had killed in the bunker were known to her personally. In a strange way, I was the intruder. Five years, after all, was a long time. Five years during which the outside world to a large extent had ceased to exist.

'Just another two names on the list, Simone.' I said. 'It's been that kind of war for me.'

She stared at me, her face white, real strain in her eyes and I knew that she wanted to say that I was different. That the Owen Morgan she had known and loved a century or two earlier was dead, another casualty of the war. But she said none of these things. Instead, she made a determined effort, smiled and took my glass.

'I'll get you some more beer.'

There were three of my father's watercolours on the wall, things he had given to the old Seigneur over the years. In particular, a view of La Grande Bay from the cliff tops on a summer's afternoon.

Steiner's easel had been moved to the far end of the room and I went towards it. Strange how neither of us had mentioned him, even obliquely, during the past half hour and yet for me, he was like a physical presence standing between us.

The painting was almost finished and was so good that it took my breath away. Even as it stood, it would have been accepted as a complete work of art anywhere. It wasn't just the technique, but the style, the sureness of touch, the feeling for form and beauty.

She appeared at my side holding the glass of beer in both hands and I said quietly. 'My father once told me that any fool could use oils, but that it took a painter to produce a water colour. This man's as good as he ever was.'

'To hear you say that would be the greatest compliment you could pay him.'

'Do you love him?'

She stared at me, eyes dark holes in the white face and I walked to the bedroom door, opened it and switched on the light. The bed had been made, but there was enough to tell me what I wanted to know. A couple of military hairbrushes on the dressing table in silver with the Brandenberg Division's crest engraved on the back, a razor, shaving brush and soap by the washbasin.

I turned and she said from the doorway, 'Five years, Owen, five years and he's a fine man. The finest I've ever known.'

'Do you love him?' I said tonelessly.

'Men,' she said it with a kind of despair in her voice. 'I speak of loneliness, or reaching out for some sort of comfort and you? For you everything has to be so simple, so neat and orderly.'

'Do you love him?' I repeated.

'How could I?' she said. 'Someone has a prior claim or had you forgotten? I was fourteen when I fell in love with you first, on your twelfth birthday as I remember.'

'You always were too old for me.'

She put a hand to my face. 'That's better, that's my Owen. It's the smile that gives you away. Little Owen Morgan—my little Owen.'

I slipped my arms about her waist and pulled her close. 'Mind your manners, girl, Colonel Morgan to you and don't forget it.'

Her eyebrows went up. 'A long way we've come from 15, New Street.'

'That was then, this is now,' I said. 'And five years is a hell of a time when you think of it.'

I could hardly claim to have been deprived of my more fleshly needs during the past few months, but the truth was that I ached for her in a way I had forgotten existed. We fell back across the bed, her mouth fastened on mine and in the distance, there was a burst of small arms fire.

I went through the living room on the run, got the door open and went outside. As I did so, there was more firing from the general direction of Charlottestown and the sinister rattle of a machine gun. A moment later, heavy diesel engines rumbled into life.

Simone appeared beside me and I said quickly, 'What's in the harbour at the moment?'

'Hardly anything,' she said. 'Mainly fishing boats left by the islanders. Oh, I'm forgetting the E-boat that came in yesterday. Just a moment, I've got some glasses in the cottage somewhere.'

An E-boat? Of all the luck. I could hear the engines very clearly now. There was more firing and then Simone appeared with a pair of binoculars in a leather case.

They were Zeiss, the very best night glasses obtainable and I didn't bother asking her where they had come from. Steiner I suppose. From La Falaise it was not possible to view the Old Harbour, but I could see the curve of the Admiralty breakwater and the entrance to what the islanders for over one hundred years had known as the New Harbour.

I focused the night glasses in time to see the E-boat move out to sea and Simone tugged at my sleeve. 'What is it, Owen? What does it mean?'

'It means everything's gone to hell,' I told her. 'Just like it says in that song of Steiner's.'

It was very much later that I was able to speak to those concerned and piece together some sort of a picture of what had happened that night.

It was Fitzgerald who was to blame, for he had most definitely acted contrary to orders. The trouble was that he and his men had found little to occupy them in the New Harbour apart from planting a few mines on fishing boats.

The strange thing is that they didn't penetrate as far as Old Harbour where they would have found the E-boat tied up to the jetty for the night, a target that would have certainly made their trip worthwhile.

Moving inshore, Fitzgerald had happened to notice a guard on an old warehouse and had decided this might well have something to do with the Nigger project. He and Grant had landed and approached the building to reconnoitre and had been immediately scented by two Alsatian guard dogs whose presence they had failed to detect. The sentry had opened fire and the whole thing had escalated from there.

The E-boat commander had certainly acted without any kind of hesitation. It must have been apparent to him the moment the dreaded cry of Commandos was raised, that the raiders must have been off-loaded in the vicinity and he would have been well aware of the type of boat used by the navy for this kind of operation.

So, the hunt was up with a vengeance now and I forgot about myself and raked the darkness out there beyond the breakwater, thinking of Dobson and his crew and the unpleasant fact that the E-boat would have ten or fifteen knots on them. And then, out there on the edge of night, a tracer flashed through the darkness in a great arc, a star shell burst and all hell broke loose.

I focused the glasses and the MGB jumped into view. I could see everything perfectly in the flash of the guns, right down to figures on the bridge and then a shell landed aft and there was a terrific explosion and she started to burn.

Simone huddled against me, an arm around my waist and I swung the glasses and caught the E-boat turning in a circle, the bit between her teeth now, hammering her adversary with everything she had.

The MGB was in a hell of a state, flames rising into the night from her stern, much of her superstructure smashed and most of her guns seemed to have stopped firing. But she still had a fair turn of speed and it was this that her commander used in the end whoever he was, although I like to think it was still Dobson.

The E-boat turned in again, closing for the kill, firing every gun she had, but this time her commander cut it just a little too close. The MGB turned into her so fast that she heeled right over. A moment later, the two boats collided, there was an enormous crash and then an explosion that rent the night, a great mushroom of fire and smoke climbing into the darkness as the fuel tanks started to go.

I could see men leaping into a sea that had become a lake of fire and lowered the glasses. Simone was crying, her face turned into my shoulder. I put an arm around her and gently led her inside.

My own prospects were anything but bright. They would certainly turn the island upside down to make sure they had laid hands on all the intruders and in such a small area the likelihood of being able to evade them for any length of time seemed slight.

The alternative had little to commend it either, which was to put to sea in the inflatable dinghy I'd left at the bottom of the Devil's Staircase and hope to make it to the French coast. There was really no choice and I tried to make that plain to Simone who didn't seem to see it that way. We had the kind of argument that is like a circle turning upon itself endlessly and it became so heated on her part that I almost missed the vehicle approaching outside.

From the sound of it, it was the VW field car which meant Steiner and that made a certain amount of sense. He would have come to explain the disturbance to her. Perhaps even to offer to stay the night.

He was already on his way to the porch, boots crunching in the gravel. She started for the door, glancing desperately at me over her shoulder and I gave her a reassuring wave and went out through the kitchen. I waited in the quiet darkness and she opened the front door and greeted him. She played her part well.

'What was it, Manfred?'

'Commandos penetrated the harbour. They seem to have been laid by the heels now, but there could be others. I think you should come into Charlottestown for the night.'

'Surely that's not necessary.' She managed a light laugh. 'They'd hardly be likely to harm me. What happened out there at sea?'

'A bad business. The E-boat moved out to search for the craft that brought them.'

'And found her?'

'They found each other, in a manner of speaking. Both gone down.'

'What about survivors?'

'Radl's ordered no craft out if that's what you mean.' He laughed bitterly. 'You know how scrupulous he is about observing the law to the very last letter and no more. It is the function of the Navy to act at sea and the E-boat was the last naval unit in Charlottestown. The Army has no jurisdiction or duty beyond the breakwater.'

'But men could be dying out there who might be saved,' she said.

'Exactly, but for Herr Colonel Otto Radl, rules are rules

and regulations are regulations.' There was a slight pause and he said in a puzzled voice. 'What's this?'

It was at that precise moment that I realised that I was not wearing my cap and I peered through the crack in the door and saw him standing near the fireplace holding it in his hands. He was dressed exactly as he had been before except that he now had a Luger pistol in a leather holster at his waist.

I felt no enmity towards this man, that was the strange thing. I knew so much about him now, I suppose. Liked and admired what I knew and had observed him with Simone who couldn't have been so hopelessly wrong in her estimate of him. Nor, for that matter, could Ezra Scully. And he could paint like an angel.

'Who has been here, Simone, you must tell me?'

His tone was more urgent now and I think, quite suddenly the possible explanation dawned on him. He started to turn and I moved through the door, the Mauser in my left hand.

'The Gestapo invented these for quiet killing and they really work so do exactly as you're told. Get his gun, Simone.'

She was pale as any ghost, eyes haunted. He stood there carved from stone, staring down at her as she moved nearer to him. She closed her eyes, shuddered and stepped back. 'No—no, Owen, I won't take sides.'

It knocked me completely off balance. I glanced towards her, Steiner pivoted on his right foot and tossed the cap into my face. In the same moment he had my left wrist, twisted the Mauser from my grasp, dropped to one knee and threw me so that I somersaulted across the carpet in the centre of the room.

I tucked in my shoulder, came up on my feet, the knife already in my right hand and brought my arm back for the throw as I turned. His reflexes were fantastic. The Luger was in his hand by a kind of magic I didn't quite understand and we both stared death in the face in that brief, brief moment. Simone drove in between us, clutching my Mauser inexpertly in one hand.

'Stop it' she screamed. 'Stop this stupid, senseless killing!' I crouched waiting, Steiner stayed on one knee, Luger ready. 'This is Owen Morgan, Manfred!' she cried. 'Don't you understand? This is Owen Morgan!'

He looked at her sharply and then at me and there was a kind of wonder in his eyes. 'This is true? You are Owen Morgan?'

'That's right.'

He smiled suddenly and unexpectedly and with quite astounding charm stood up and pushed the Luger back into its holster. Then he put an arm around her. 'It's all right, Simone. Everything will be all right now.'

He tried to take the Mauser from her hand and she backed away from him. 'No, I'm keeping this for the moment. I hold the balance, is that understood? I won't have either of you hurt. I won't stand for it.'

She stared at us wildly, turned and rushed into the bedroom. The door banged and Steiner shook his head and sighed. 'Poor Simone. War is difficult enough at the best of times, but when you don't want to take sides . . .' He held out a hand. 'Manfred Steiner. I've wanted to meet you for quite a while now. The famous Owen Morgan.'

'I didn't realise I was that quite.'

'From Simone it is Owen Morgan from morning to night. Every rock on every shore seems to be a monument to something you did together, some fabulous exploit from the endless summer.'

I gave him a cigarette and he eyed me speculatively. 'You came with the Commandos?'

I saw no reason to deny it. 'I was in command of the overall operation.'

'But not in uniform.'

I shrugged. 'In uniform or out, what does it matter where the Kommandobefehl holds.'

'And it holds here, I warn you,' he said. 'The acting governor, Colonel Radl, is a hard man. The kind who believes in obeying orders, however unpleasant and standing orders still lay down that special service troops of any description when captured are to be executed as soon as possible and that the Commander in each area will be held personally responsible to see that the order is obeyed to the letter.'

'A foolish action on Radl's part, surely,' I said. 'The war can't last more than another month at the most. In case you don't know it, British troops are about to cross the Elbe and the Russians are battering at the gates of Berlin.'

'I'm aware of that,' he said. 'I probably listen to the

B.B.C. more frequently than you do, but Radl is a special kind of man. He was with Hitler as a young man back in the twenties before the Party's rise to power. For him it takes the place of a religion. He believes utterly and completely. He would face his own execution, die for his own faith as tranquilly as an early Christian martyred for Christ's sake in a Roman arena. Nothing could persuade him to change his mind.'

'How many of the raiding party survived?'

'I don't know. There are certainly prisoners. Two at least. I was told as much by a Pioneer Corporal on his way to the Platzkommandantur with the news.' He shook his head. 'What point was there to it?'

'We were after you as a matter of fact and your Nigger installation.' I sat on the edge of the table. 'The powers-that-be decided you might be a threat if your people decide to fight in the Channel Islands instead of surrendering.'

'The Nigger installation?' He was genuinely astonished, then burst into a roar of laughter. 'The Nigger installation a threat? That's the funniest thing I've heard in years. There *is* no Nigger installation. Hasn't been for something like two months now which was when we used our last torpedoes.' He laughed again and shook his head. 'For us the war is over or was until this little affair tonight. When the war ends in Germany it will end here too, I promise you.'

'Which still leaves us with Colonel Radl and his S.S. paratroopers and the situation here.' Simone stood in the bedroom doorway. 'What happens if he lays hands on Owen?'

And we all knew the answer to that one. 'Rather awkward now that you can't be picked up.' Steiner said, 'Have you anything else in mind?'

'I left an inflatable dinghy back there when I landed. I could try for France.'

'A long shot.'

'Better than staying here. Am I to presume you won't interfere?'

'I don't have much choice in the matter, do I?' He nodded towards Simone. 'As far as I am concerned, you haven't even been here. Have you any idea how the S.S. would treat her if they suspected you'd had any contact?'

'I certainly have,' I said. 'Perhaps more so than you, but that's another story.'

I checked my watch. The exit hole at the bottom of the Devil's Staircase would still be under four or five feet of water, but the level would drop rapidly within the next hour or so. There was really very little point in continuing here.

I picked up my cap, pulled it on and moved to the easel. 'I like your work. There's nothing quite like a good water colour.'

'The only medium as far as I am concerned.'

'You'd have got on with my father, I can see that. You have the same trick of soaking one colour into another in the background washes. I've never noticed it in any other artist but him.'

'Ah, but now you are talking about a painter,' he said. 'A genius. When I was at the Slade, he was a legend. The island fisherman who'd never had a formal lesson in his life. Do you know, quite small examples of his works were changing hands at five hundred guineas a time and I'm speaking of 1935. And the manner of his death. Remarkable. Not many men become legends in so short a time.'

There was an awkward silence as we stood there, he in his uniform with all the medals and me dressed like a bosun off a Finnish windjammer and I liked him more than any man I'd known in all those long years since my father's death. Liked him instinctively and for no particular reason I was prepared to state.

Simone came forward and thrust my Mauser into my hand. 'Go on—get out of it! Go to your death if that's what you want. Look at you, the two of you standing there with nothing to say because there is nothing to say. It's all too stupid for words. Beyond belief.'

She burst into tears and flung herself down on the couch. Steiner held out his hand. 'Goodbye, Owen Morgan. I would like to have known you better, but the war, as always, has a habit of getting into the way of things.'

I nodded briefly. 'Look after her, won't you?'

He nodded and I turned and went out.

It took me no more than half an hour to work my way across to the road that led down to the bunker above the

Devil's Staircase. I heard voices when I was still a hundred yards or more away from it and jumped for a ditch as a halftrack troop carrier roared out of the night from the direction of Fort Marie Louise.

There was all kinds of activity down there around the bunker and after a while another vehicle arrived and I heard dogs snarling angrily. That did it. I moved out fast and set off across the fields in the general direction of Granville. Progress was slow because on several occasions I found myself caught in the barbed wire defensive system and the possibility of mines to go with them put my teeth on edge.

There was a kind of inevitability to it all. It wasn't just that I was in trouble. There was much more to it than that. I was caught in some web of events with a part still to play, I knew that with complete and utter certainty.

There was no chance that I could reach Granville before dawn and even if I did, where would I go? No, I needed a place no one would ever suspect and remembered the cliffs above Horseshoe where I had played as a boy with Simone, a secret hiding place half-way down at a seemingly inaccessible spot.

I had some difficulty finding it in the dark, but finally made it in one piece, scratched and bruised, and squatted under an overhang of rock on a small ledge surrounded by gorse bushes. If I could hide throughout the daylight hours there was just a chance, just one slim chance that they might think they had accounted for everyone and would call off the search.

I crouched there and waited as light gradually seeped into the darkness on the edge of the world. Down there in the bay, the bodies started to come in with the tide just after dawn, clustered together, bobbing in through the surf to the beach a hundred feet below my hiding place.

8   A Land of Standing Corpses

That Radl had miscalculated the nature of the operation only became apparent later that morning when the door of the old ammunition store was unlocked and a couple of

his S.S. paratroopers appeared. They didn't look too
pleased and ordered us out pretty sharply. A half-track
troop carrier was waiting in the courtyard and we were
pushed on board without ceremony and driven to the harbour.

There seemed to be plenty of people about down there
one way and another. Thirty or forty German troops to
start with, all Pioneers and about the same number of
Todt workers shivering in their ragged clothes as they
huddled against the wall in an attempt to get some shelter
from the driving rain.

The harbour was exactly as I remembered except for
the more obvious scars left by the bombing raids of the
past and the naval bombardment of the previous year.
There were about twenty fishing boats of various sizes and
types anchored in the lee of the breakwater and out in the
centre of New Harbour, the funnel of an armed German
trawler just showed above the surface. She had been sunk
by bombs at her moorings eighteen months previously,
something else Joe St Martin had failed to mention.

I saw Steiner on the lower jetty as I got out of the
troop carrier. He was wearing a frogman's suit of black
rubber and there were four other men with him in the
same rig. They were all Brandenbergers, all that survived
of the original group which had manned the Nigger installation.

They had two of the Rob Roy canoes on the jetty, obviously salvaged from the harbour for Fitzgerald and his
men had followed the usual procedure of sinking them together with all their equipment when faced with capture.

Half-a-dozen limpet mines were laid out in a neat line
and the Brandenbergers were apparently de-fusing them
there and then. They had the manner of all special service
troops everywhere in any army. That easy arrogance that
is not arrogance, but something quite indefinable that
comes from a belief in one's own self-sufficiency, a pro-
duct of the constant danger in which such men lived their
lives. In those rubber suits they could have as easily been
British Commandos or American Rangers. Only the conversation drifting up through the rain indicated their nationality.

I got to know them all well in the time that followed
that first day. Lanz and Obermeyer, the two sergeants who

had been music students together in Berlin before the war. Corporal Hilldorf who had been a schoolteacher in a village near Hamburg and Schreiber who had worked in a bank in Vienna, but only because he had not been able to make a living out of his writing.

Lanz crouched, a cigarette dangling from his lips as he delicately removed a fuse from one of the mines. Obermeyer made a remark I couldn't quite catch, but there was a burst of laughter. Steiner turned round and saw me and said something. Lanz glanced up, a slight smile on his face, then gave his attention to the next mine. Everyone else was standing well back for obvious reasons and I noticed Major Brandt watching at the edge of the crowd. He turned casually, saw us and came forward.

He saluted formally. 'Good morning, Colonel.'

'What are we here for?' I asked.

'Colonel Radl's orders. He will be here himself soon.' He nodded towards the group on the lower jetty as more light laughter floated up. 'These Brandenbergers—crazy.' He tapped his head. 'One of them is sufficient for such a job and yet the others have to keep him company. One mistake and they all go up in smoke. Why?'

'If I have to explain, then you wouldn't understand anyway.'

I produced my tin of cigarettes. There were only eight left now. I lit one, flicked the match away and walked across to the steps leading down to the lower jetty, my chain clinking musically. Why did I do it? I don't really know. Some kind of gesture, I suppose. A challenge to authority or perhaps, just the impulse of the moment.

There was a harsh, metallic click as a machine pistol was cocked by one of the S.S. paratroopers and Brandt called urgently. 'Please, Colonel Morgan! Stay where you are!'

I paused a yard or two away from the edge and glanced back. The S.S. man had his machine pistol trained on me and looked as if he was quite prepared to use it.

'If you think I'm likely to escape, better let him shoot,' I called to Brandt. 'It comes to the same thing in the end. On the other hand, I'm hardly likely to get far with a couple of feet of chain between my ankles.'

I moved to the steps and Brandt said crisply in German, 'No, let him go!'

I went down with care for I was still inclined to mis-judge what leeway the chain allowed and a stumble here could well mean a broken neck. I was half-way down when Fitzgerald appeared above me.

I waited at the bottom and when he reached me, he said calmly, 'Join you if I may, sir. I told the others to stay where they are.'

I looked up as Grant and Hagen appeared at the top of the steps. 'I always did say you Yanks had no discipline.'

He smiled at that with something like warmth for the first time since I had known him and there was a strange light in his eyes. 'You're not afraid at all, are you? Not one damned bit.'

'As you Americans would say, there's no percentage in it,' I said. 'Here's another bit of Wu'chi for you. The field of battle is a land of standing corpses. Those determined to die will live. Those who hope to escape with their lives will die.'

I don't think he really understood, but he was prepared to accept it as just another of my eccentricities. 'Shall we join the party, then?' he said.

He had difficulty in holding down his excitement and for the first time I think I fully understood him, or as much as one can ever hope to understand anyone. I had come down to the jetty for no sensible reason known to man, for no reasonable man would ever have done such a thing.

Fitzgerald, on the other hand, saw it as a heroic ges-ture. High drama. Brave men facing death gallantly and not caring. I realised then, and my suspicions were to be utterly confirmed by what happened later, that for him, war *was* something brave and heroic and splendid. I had told Henry that to me, he looked the sort who wanted to die sabre in hand, bugles blowing faintly on the wind. I had not been far off the mark.

Steiner waited for us, hands on hips, his men grouped behind him except for Lanz who crouched where he was, a mine between his feet.

'Morning,' I called in German as we approached. 'Hav-ing fun?'

Steiner grinned and said something over his shoulder to his men. 'Depends on your point of view,' he called back. 'A new model. Lanz is finding the fuse box cover tricky.'

Lanz's cigarette had gone out and hung from his lower lip. His face was impassive, but the tendons showed clearly in the back of the right hand as he tried to rotate the box cover. Grant arrived at that precise moment with the other three Rangers and we all stood watching. It was Sergeant Hagen who started it off.

'What's he trying to do, for Christ's sake? Blow us all up or something?' He squatted beside Lanz and put a hand on his arm. 'Not the way, buddy. Let me.'

Fitzgerald made no attempt to stop him and Hagen turned gently and lifted. 'It's all in feeling for the coil spring at just the right point. I guess you were lucky with the first one.'

The cover came out and as he held it, Lanz gently withdrew the fuse. The German grinned and slapped the American on the shoulder. After that, everyone had to get in on the act including Fitzgerald.

I stood watching them crouched there on the cobbles together, Brandenbergers and Rangers and Steiner joined me. 'You are familiar with Alice in Wonderland?'

'I know,' I said. 'Curiouser and curiouser, said Alice. It certainly makes you think.'

We moved a couple of yards away from the others. 'There's no question of Simone being questioned?' I asked him in a low voice. 'You're certain?'

He shook his head. 'I told Radl she was in my company. That's what he meant when he said you couldn't have contacted any islanders last night because one way or another they were all under surveillance.'

There was a sudden shout, we turned and saw Radl at the top of the steps. 'What's going on down there, Steiner?' he called. 'Bring the prisoners up at once.'

It was Fitzgerald who answered and in excellent German, which came as a surprise as he had not seen fit to mention his ability in that direction. 'Maybe a little later, Colonel, we're rather busy at the moment.'

He gave his attention to the limpet mine he was holding. Radl stood looking down at us all for a moment, then descended the steps slowly. Presumably he was proving either to himself or the crowd up there, that whatever we could do, he could. Brandt followed him with reluctance, his face pale, which only proved that he had the good sense to be scared. As they joined us, Hagen removed the last fuse and the whole group, Germans and Americans alike, gave a ragged cheer. Radl watched with no visible emotion, then turned to me.

'I made a grave error last night, Colonel Morgan, in assuming that the sole purpose of the raid was to attack targets on land. You will tell me now, please, which boats in the harbour have been mined.'

Fitzgerald took a step forward. 'You're talking to the wrong man, Colonel. I was in charge of the harbour operation.'

'Then you will give me the information I require.'

There was a heavy silence. Grant understood a little German, but the other Rangers were completely in the dark. The Brandenbergers all looked serious, I suppose because they knew Radl and expected the worst from him.

'Well now, Colonel,' Fitzgerald said. 'I don't really see my way clear to doing that.'

The situation was quite farcical. He and his men had fixed their mines to several fishing boats for want of better targets. Boats that were not even in use. It would harm no one, but their unfortunate owners now exiled to Guernsey, to send them to the bottom. But for a man like Fitzgerald, it was a question of principle, whatever that was supposed to mean and the fact that he had just spent ten minutes helping to de-fuse the mines brought up from the harbour bottom by the Brandenbergers, had nothing to do with it.

For Radl, too, it was a matter of principle which in his case probably came down to the determination not to lose face. There was a fair crowd up there on the harbour wall now and they weren't going to see a dozen fishing boats blow up one after the other if he could help it.

He turned to me. 'Colonel Morgan, as Major Fitzgerald's senior officer . . .'

'No use appealing to me on this one,' I told him. 'As Major Fitzgerald says, he was in charge of the harbour.'

'Very well. You leave me no choice.' He turned to Brandt. 'By my reckoning, there are twenty-three boats in the harbour. Round up as many Todt workers as you can find in the vicinity. We'll have two or three on each boat.'

It was a rather obvious ploy and in a similar situation, I'd probably have done exactly the same. So far as Fitzgerald was concerned, it took a moment or two for it to sink in, but when it did, his face turned pale. 'Does he

mean what I think he means?' he demanded, a hand on
my arm.

'I would imagine so.'

I suppose it was the unfairness of it that hurt him most
of all. The fact that Radl was winning by underhand
methods. Any moment now I expected him to burst out
with an immortal remark on the lines of: 'But good God,
man, it isn't war.'

Instead he suddenly looked rather tired. 'Okay, Colonel,
you win. We attached mines to five of the boats out there.
They were timed for ten o'clock, which doesn't give us
more than half an hour, so we'd better get moving if
we're going to do anything about it.'

They used the two Rob Roy canoes with a Brandenberger and a Ranger in each to retrieve the mines and Radl
stood at the edge of the jetty and watched.

'Today's comforting thought,' I said to Steiner. 'If anything blows, we all go together, including him.'

'We have a saying,' he said. 'Some good in every mis-
fortune.'

Radl produced a cigarette case, selected a long black
Russian cigarette, the kind that is half cardboard tube.
One of his men, a sergeant, moved in smoothly and offered him a light. Radl took it without even looking at the
man and stood there, flicking one glove against his thigh
as he watched proceedings in the harbour.

'Every inch a soldier,' I commented softly.

'Or every inch of what he thinks a soldier should look
like,' Steiner said. 'He was an infantry corporal in 1918, a
railway clerk for several years after that. Rank means a
lot to him. Appearances are important. The Russian cigarettes, for example, are to tell you he was on the Eastern
Front, an affectation of at least one of our better known
generals. But he makes mistakes. A gentleman would have
thanked the sergeant who gave him the light and the uniform is just a shade too perfect. All right for the opera—
on stage, of course, which sums him up rather well. An
indifferent actor in the wrong role. Bad casting.'

'I suspect he'd say that of you,' I said, 'which probably
explains why he dislikes you. Your own casting isn't exactly perfect. He probably has to restrain himself from
saluting you first.'

'What he can't understand, he fears,' Steiner said. 'The Party is everything to his kind. It is all he has. All he has ever had.'

'And what does a man like him do after the war?' I asked. 'What kind of future is there for him?'

He turned, his face serious. 'For him, there is no future, my friend. You would do well to remember that.'

I took his point. 'How long before the new governor arrives?'

'Captain Olbricht? I'm not sure. He's quite the hero, you know. A big U-boat ace. He was badly wounded last year which put an end to active sea duty for him. We're expecting an armed coaster to attempt the blockade from St Denise with ammunition and supplies. An old tub called the *Pride of Hamburg*. He's supposed to be coming with her.'

'She's not left yet?'

He shook his head. 'Something called the Royal Navy can prove rather awkward in these waters. The captain of the *Pride of Hamburg* is an old salt called Ritter. I know him well. He usually waits for dirty weather and uses it as cover.'

'Let's hope it stays fine for him for the next week or so.'

'And for you, my friend.'

He left me and went to join Fitzgerald and the others as the first canoe returned with its mines. I watched for a moment, then turned and started to shuffle away. Nothing was going to happen. No one was going to get blown to Kingdom Come.

Radl called, 'Had enough, Colonel Morgan?'

'Something like that. I'll go back up if you have no objection.'

'But of course not.'

He was smiling, secure in the knowledge that I had broken in some way that he had not. He turned and whistling cheerfully, crossed to the group working on the mines and stood watching them. Brandt followed me up the steps and the crowd of soldiers at the top moved back when he ordered them to sharply.

'Owen? Owen Morgan? Is that you?'

Paddy Riley, the island doctor pushed his way through the press. He must have been at least seventy, a tall, white-haired Irishman with an untidy beard who had never lost his accent. He pumped my hand up and down, smiling hugely, yet there was something in his eyes, something that told me he knew more than he was able to say.

I realised what the game was when he turned and called, 'Simone. I've found him.'

She appeared from the crowd wearing a headscarf and old trenchcoat and came towards me, her face serious. She held out a hand hesitantly and I took it. 'Hello, Owen,' she said. 'I'm sorry to see you in such circumstances.'

'Good morning, Miss de Beaumarchais.' Radl looked on the scene and clicked his heels in the approved manner.

'Simone and I are old friends,' I told him.

'Indeed?'

She looked as if she might burst into tears at any moment and Riley put an arm around her shoulders. 'Come on now, my dear, I'll take you back to the hospital. You'll only distress yourself here.'

She turned without a word and walked away. Riley said to me, 'Anything I can do for you, just let me know. I'm the only doctor they've got so they damn well have to be nice to me. On top of that I'm still a citizen of the Republic of Ireland which I don't let some people forget.'

He scowled at Radl and went after Simone. The German smiled, 'The Irish are a strange people. Always boiling over about something.'

I didn't bother answering and at that moment, a motor cyclist arrived with some sort of message for him. I turned and noticed Ezra watching me. There was a German with him in a uniform with a distinct nautical flavour to it.

'Ezra,' I called. 'Ezra Scully, you old devil. How are you? It must be all of five years.'

He played up well and came and shook hands. 'I heard you were with this party, Owen,' he said. 'Sergeant-Major Steiner told me.'

I nodded. 'I didn't think you'd still be here.'

'Oh, aye, they needed a harbour pilot see? This here is Captain Warger, Wilhelm Warger, the harbourmaster, though there's precious little for him to do these days.'

I nodded to Warger who insisted on shaking hands. 'A pleasure, Colonel Morgan,' he said in his precise, stiff English. 'I have seen your name on the lifeboat here.'

'My father's,' I corrected him, and said to Ezra, 'It's still here then?'

He nodded solemnly. 'In the boathouse at Granville. Can't get it out. Someone dropped a bomb on the slipway years back.'

There was an awkward silence and then Fitzgerald appeared at the top of the steps. He looked tired, from strain, I think, rather than for any physical reason. As he came towards me, Radl joined us.

'Everything in order?'

Fitzgerald nodded wearily without saying anything and the others came up the steps from the jetty behind him, Rangers and Brandenbergers together, Steiner in the lead.

Radl looked them over calmly, then said to Brandt who was standing nearby. 'You will return Colonel Morgan and his men to the fort. Feed them, then set them to work. The road gang, I think, will do very well for the moment.

Which was letting us all know exactly where we stood including Steiner and his Brandenbergers. Radl saluted me formally, walked to his Mercedes and was driven away.

9 The Road Gang

The first day on the road gang was hard and for me most of all. The period in hospital, the months of idleness in Cornwall had taken their toll and I was no longer in particularly good physical condition, unlike Fitzgerald and his Rangers who seemed to take twelve hours a day with a pick and shovel in their stride.

Considering the circumstances, they were all remarkably cheerful, but the reason was simple enough. Not one of them, including Fitzgerald, believed for a moment that there was any prospect of the executions promised by Radl taking place. The war might end any day and only a madman would be willing to take responsibility at this stage for an act that would surely sign his own death warrant afterwards.

From what I had seen of Radl, I wasn't too happy

about that line of argument and it seemed to me then that our strongest chance of survival lay in the fact that it was highly unlikely that Olbricht, the new governor, would ever manage to get to St Pierre from Brittany at all through the kind of blockade the Navy was putting up at that time.

There was always the possibility of escape, of course, and it had been thoroughly discussed, but at the moment, there didn't seem to be much hope in that direction. It wasn't just the chains or the constant armed guards. It was the simple fact that having broken free, there would be nowhere to run. On such a small island it would be impossible to remain at large for very long and the place had been turned into an impregnable fortress so far as I could see, every cliff and headland boasting artillery positions, machine gun posts and concrete bunkers of one kind or another. Since the raid, all guards had been doubled.

So, for the moment, we worked and made the best of things and waited for something to happen or at least I did, for out of some strange sixth sense, I was aware that we stood on the brink of events and waited, sniffing at the weather, glancing often at the sky, a slight aching pressure behind the eyes, wary as any animal that senses thunder beyond the horizon. Yet even I could not have guessed at the extraordinary course things were to take.

Whatever the calendar says, the first day of spring is never a question of date. Day follows day, much as usual and the world waits and then it happens. A morning to thank God for. A morning of blue skies and soft air and scents and sounds that all winter long one has forgotten existed.

In the spring, there is nowhere quite like St Pierre with the blackthorn blossom like snow in the hollows and the cliffs draped in sea campion, thrift and broom, the yellows and mauves and whites so vivid that the sight of them catches at the throat.

On the fourth morning, working up there on the spine of the island with a view that encompassed most of it, I was glad to be alive and one with all this beauty—glad in a new and disturbing way. Perhaps it was being here in this place that held so many memories of childhood and young manhood for me—memories that turned me over

like some great sea rolling in down there, bringing to the
surface glimpses of that other, different Owen Morgan
who had existed here so long ago.

I swung the ten pound hammer high above my head
and brought it down with all my force, splitting the stone
in front of me, then rested for a moment, wiping sweat
from my forehead with the back of a hand.

There were thirty of us in all, the rest being Todt workers and the half-dozen Pioneers with their machine pistols
were in our honour, not theirs, for usually Todt workers
were not guarded—not on St Pierre. They were as sorry a
lot as I had seen in many a long day, their clothes in rags,
the flesh on their faces so tight that every bone showed
clearly.

Not that the Pioneers looked particularly well fed for
since the Normandy landings, food had been scarce in the
Channel Islands. They were commanded by a sergeant
called Braun, one of the three I had seen playing cards
with Ezra at his cottage. Whether Ezra had spoken to him
about me, I did not know, but he certainly went out of his
way to be kind and he and his men treated us all with respect.

The road was to follow the course of an old farm track
to a point on the coast below Fort Marie Louise. Apparently there were plans for a new heavy gun emplacement
there. They were certainly working right up to the bitter
end, one had to give them that.

It was mid-morning when Steiner arrived in a field car.
He was in uniform and wore the Russian staff officer's
coat with the fur collar. Sergeant Braun couldn't have
given Colonel Radl a better reception. Even allowing for
the fact that warrant officers in the German army had far
higher status than in any other within my experience,
there was little doubt that Steiner seemed to command extraordinary respect from everyone, including the officers.

He produced a slip of paper which he showed to Braun
who nodded at once and Steiner crossed to where I was
working. 'Colonel Morgan, you will come with me.'

Fitzgerald turned sharply, leaning on his shovel, a
frown on his face and further on down the line, the other
Rangers paused also. 'What is this?' Fitzgerald demanded.

There was a certain anxiety in his voice, which made
sense. For all he knew, I was being taken away to face

some kind of interrogation or other unpleasantness. He knew nothing of my meeting with Simone and of my special relationship with Steiner, for the simple reason that I had chosen not to tell him. If I had learnt one thing in this war it was the undeniable fact that somewhere along the line each man had his breaking point. We had one golden rule above all others in the Resistance which was quite simply that what you didn't know, you couldn't tell. It had saved more lives than one from betrayal to my certain knowledge.

'There is no cause for alarm,' Steiner said.

Which I knew anyway and nodded to Fitzgerald. 'Don't worry, it's going to be all right.'

I climbed into the passenger seat of the VW with difficulty because of my chains and Steiner got behind the wheel and drove away. We took the road down towards the Devil's Staircase, the road I had followed that first night.

'What's it all about?' I asked.

'Simone wants to see you.'

I was aware of a quickening of the pulse. 'How did you manage it?'

He took a paper from his pocket and passed it across. It stated that I was to be released into Sergeant-Major Steiner's care for the purpose of assisting him with my local knowledge on a beach survey. It was signed by a Captain Heinz Schellenberg of the 271st Pioneer Regiment.

'Is it genuine?' I demanded.

'They have to find me something to do so each day I examine beach defences, check upon what inroads the sea has made. Sometimes there is work that only frogmen can do. In such cases, any information you would be willing to give about local tidal conditions would be invaluable. These are extraordinarily dangerous waters.'

He delivered all this with a perfectly straight face and I said, 'Schellenberg fell for that?'

'He used to work for my step-father,' Steiner said tranquilly. 'Along with half the population of Germany at a rough estimate. He would like to work for him again. I'm afraid that I allowed him to think that I might have some influence in that direction.'

'And have you?'

He smiled. 'As long as my mother lives. The one piece

of good taste he has ever shown was to fall in love with her and stay in love. For her sake he puts up with me and such eccentricities as my refusal to take a commission. On the other hand, my Knight's Cross sent him into raptures, particularly when the Fuhrer sent a personal message of congratulations—to him, not me.'

'The war ends any day now,' I reminded him. 'And your side lost. Where does that leave your father?'

'Where it has always done. With several millions of dollars deposited in various Swiss banks, with industrial interests throughout most of the world, including Great Britain and America through subsidiary companies. The meek,' he added with considerable irony, 'shall inherit the earth.'

'You don't sound too upset.'

'Why should I? There was a time when I took it all very seriously. I wasn't a Nazi—try not to laugh—but I was a German and my country was at war. Friends of mine were facing great danger, dying on occasion. I compromised by playing my part as a private soldier.'

'Killing without having the responsibility for it?' I commented. 'It's a point of view.'

'You don't approve?' He shrugged. 'It doesn't matter. I volunteered for the Brandenberg Division because special service work seemed to offer some kind of solution. One is at risk more often, fate has a direct responsibility for the length of time one survives. Does that make sense?'

'To me, but then I'm as crazy as you are from the sound of it.'

'I made, what was for me, a truly amazing discovery,' he said. 'Men die or get wounded or crippled for life for the same reason it rains for every day of the fortnight's holiday that some poor wretch has saved for, and looked forward to, for the whole of a working year. Things happen because they happen. No reason. No reason at all.'

'Alles est veruckt,' I quoted softly. 'Everything's crazy. Everything's gone to hell. I think some of that Russian cold got into your brain, my friend.'

His face was—how shall I describe it?—suddenly desolate. 'More than that,' he replied bitterly. 'It touched the heart, Owen Morgan, and that is death in life. Have you seen corpses walk?' He shivered. 'Will any of us who were there ever forget Russia?'

There was a shadow between us then that for the moment could not be blown away and we continued in silence.

La Grande Bay from that day on became Steiner's bay for me and in all the years that have followed, I have found it impossible to think of it any differently.

It lay at the bottom of three hundred feet cliffs, a horseshoe of white sand slipping into green-blue water. Beyond, a rocky islet or two shone in the sun. The seaweed on the lower flanks still wet for the tide was on the ebb.

It was reached by a narrow path fit only for goats, that zig-zagged across the face of the cliffs and was no place for the faint-hearted. We braked to a halt a foot or two away from a notice that warned of mines.

'Where are we going?' I asked Steiner.

'Get out, I'll show you.'

The view from the edge of the cliff was breath-taking. The sun sparkled on the water and on the other side of the barbed wire below, the white sand eased itself into a sea that even the Mediterranean would have had difficulty in improving on.

Simone was swimming down there or at least I presumed it was Simone. I turned and pointed to the warning notice.

'What about this?'

Steiner smiled. 'The engineer officer in charge of minelaying back in 1940 fell in love with this beach to such an extent that he couldn't bear to mine it. He put up the notice and the barbed wire to make it look good. He used to go for early morning swims and got drunk one night and told Ezra Scully his shameful secret. Ezra, who is by way of being a friend of mine, told me.'

I couldn't help laughing and when he looked puzzled, explained. It had him smiling again. 'Now *that* really does restore my faith in human nature. Shall we go down?'

I swung my legs awkwardly to the ground and he came round from the other side, produced a key, knelt down and unlocked my irons. 'Better to carry them,' he said briefly.

There was no question of asking for my parole, I think he would have thought it an insult to ask. I liked him for that, but then I was beginning to like him for a lot of things.

The path had deteriorated since my day when concrete steps had been built into the more dangerous sections for the benefit of the tourists.

Now even the concrete had crumbled and whole sections of the path had ceased to exist so that it was necessary to take it very cautiously indeed.

Gulls cried high in the sky and rose and fell in swarms from their nesting places on the cliff ledges and below, the surf boiled in like white smoke. Half-way down I paused to watch her. She was wearing a black bathing costume and her long dark hair was covered by a rubber bathing cap so that planing in through the surf, she might have been some legendary sea-beast, half-seal, half-woman.

'She's quite a girl, isn't she?' he said from behind.

I turned and put it to him directly. 'You love her, don't you?'

'But of course. How could it be otherwise?'

'And what about her?'

'I think she is too easily held by old loyalties.' He smiled. 'But then, you could say that I am prejudiced.'

'To put it mildly,' I observed and started down again.

I should have been angry or dismayed a little at his confidence if nothing else. The trouble was that I liked the man which put me in a difficult position. And Simone? What did she want? Really want more than anything else in the world?

I dropped the last few feet into soft sand and moved across the beach as she came in on the next big one, head down, arms out in front of her. She disappeared in a welter of foam that left her high and dry when it receded.

She got to her feet laughing and ran up the beach before the next one could catch her, tugging at her bathing cap. As it came off, the dark hair fell in a curtain on either side of her face.

She paused for a moment at the sight of me, then smiled and came on, a hand outstretched. 'Oh, Owen, it is good to see you again.'

It seemed genuine enough, but when I leaned forward to kiss her lightly on the forehead there was a stiffening that was almost imperceptible.

Her towel was on a rock a few yards away together

with an old beach robe. She pulled it on and started to
dry her legs. 'So Manfred managed to pull it off?'

'He certainly seems to have influence,' I said.

She nodded. 'In most things, but I wasn't too certain
this time. I was sure Radl would prove difficult.'

'To the best of my knowledge he doesn't know the first
thing about it.' I turned, looking for Steiner and found
him gone. 'Where is he?'

'Getting his painting things from one of the caves. He
keeps an easel down here permanently.'

'He paints a lot then?'

She nodded. 'Particularly down here. He loves it.'

'Among other things.'

Her face darkened and she looked not only uncertain,
but quite miserable. My heart went out to her and I produced my waterproof tin of cigarettes—old faithful. I had
been taking it very steadily and there were still three left.

'Don't take any notice of me, it's been a long war. Have
one of these.'

I held out the tin. She glanced inside and shook her
head. 'I'll share one with you.'

Which was a companionable thing to do. Steiner appeared from among the mass of great boulders that
sprawled at the base of the cliff carrying an easel and a
wooden case. I watched him setting things up and was reminded with something like nostalgia, of Mary Barton and
that beach near Lizard Point. *Dear Mary.* I wondered
what she was doing at this precise moment. Crying, perhaps, over poor Owen Morgan, for Henry, I was certain,
would have been to see her with some sort of sorry news
by now.

Simone reached for my cigarette and inhaled. She
handed it back, her face grave. 'Is it very bad, Owen?'

'The road gang?' I shook my head. 'The guards are decent enough. Today it's a Pioneer Sergeant called Braun
in charge. He alternates with Sergeant Schmidt. They are
both cronies of Ezra.'

She smiled briefly. 'Yes, I know, they've been here four
years now.'

And then there was silence between us. I lay on my
back and looked up at the cloudless sky and smoked my
cigarette. After a while, she said hesitantly, 'It's all going
to come out all right, Owen, do you realise that?'

'Is it?'

'Of course it is,' she said eagerly. 'Manfred says Radl is a man who lives by the book. If it is in the regulations, he does it, but if it isn't . . .'

'A comforting thought.'

Perhaps I sounded sceptical for she dropped to the sand beside me and said insistently, 'But it's true. The commanding officer in each sector is the only person with the authority to carry out the Kommandobefehl and Radl is only acting governor here. The war could be over any day now according to the B.B.C. The Russians are fighting in the suburbs of Berlin. Olbricht will never get here now.'

'I suppose Steiner told you that also?'

She started to frown, then checked it, obviously making a determined effort to cope with my petulance. 'Even if Olbricht did get here, he would never carry out such an execution at this stage in the war. It would be unthinkable.'

'Steiner again?' I demanded.

She struck at me blindly so that I had to catch her wrists to fend her off. 'Damn you, Owen Morgan!' she raged and for the first time, became again the girl I had known before the war. 'Damn you to hell! Why did you have to come back like this? Why couldn't you have waited?'

'Don't you mean why did I have to come back at all?'

I was on my feet now and dragging her up with me. I shook her angrily. 'You're in love with him, aren't you? For God's sake be honest about it.'

She stared up at me and somewhere, I heard Steiner cry out and then she laughed wildly. 'All right, if you want the truth. I'm in love with Manfred and I'm afraid of you—you and that damned knife of yours and of what you've become. I think of those two wretched sentries you killed and I find myself hating you and then see you like this, hear your voice and remember so many things and love comes up through all the fear and the hating.' She was crying now. 'So I still love you, Owen, that's the one thing I can't escape from. I love you and I love Manfred. Now what would you suggest that I do about that?'

She turned and ran and kept on running, avoiding Steiner's outstretched hand until she reached the bottom of the path and started to climb. 'What went wrong?' he demanded.

'Was anything supposed to go right?' He frowned and for the first time since I'd known him looked as if he could be angry. I raised a hand between us and sighed wearily. 'Forget I said that. You meant well. What were you trying to do, make the great sacrifice of your life?'

'Something like that.' He smiled briefly and then was serious again. 'Why did she become so upset?'

'Because she's decided she's in love with two men at once.'

'And you believe that?'

'She does, that's the important thing. She loves you and she loves me at the same time and if that isn't complicated enough for you, she's also afraid of me—me and my knife, that is.'

There was something like amusement in his eyes, but more than that—a kind of relief. 'I see.'

'If you do, you're a better man than I am,' I said sourly and walked across to his easel.

He was working on a view of the east headland and a shaft of rock a hundred yards out to sea beyond that was a favourite nesting place for puffins. There was no basic sketch in pencil or charcoal. The entire thing was developed purely in paint, delicate washes of colour soaking into each other and his sea was particularly fine. The whole picture had a quality of real emotion to it and reminded me strongly of my father's work as had his painting of Simone.

'I like the way you soak one layer of colour into another,' I said. 'The surf is about twenty-seven different shades of white and you've got them all. My father did a view of the harbour and breakwater with the sea coming over it in which he employed the same technique. Simone's father bought it, as I remember.'

'It still hangs on the wall of the study at the Seigneurie,' he said. 'Although Patrick Riley uses that as his office now. I have examined that painting many times. I think I learned more about water colour technique from it than I did during the whole time I studied in London and Paris. He was a master, your father. A great master.'

To have thanked him for that would have been rather superfluous. He sat down at his easel and went back to work and I lay in the sun and we talked about my father and painting and art generally and women and drink and most things in between.

I don't think I'd had such a conversation with anyone in years, for in my line of work, close relationships had been undersirable. It was very pleasant lying there in the sun and after a while he seemed to stop talking and I drifted into sleep.

A gull cried high above my head, harsh, insistent, and I sat up with a start. Steiner was nowhere to be seen. For a moment I had the strange cold feeling that it might all be a dream, that I was back on some boyhood beach and everything else had been simply a memory from the half-world of dreams. And then Steiner came out of the cave beyond the rocks and I realised that he had simply been putting his equipment away again.

'So you are awake? Time to go now.'

'Thanks for the party,' I said. 'I enjoyed the conversation. As for the other business . . . let's just say you meant well and leave it at that.'

He didn't reply. In fact, I didn't give him the chance because I turned away, crossed to where the path began and started to scramble to the top. It was damned hard going, but I didn't really notice for I had other things on my mind. Steiner, because I liked him and Simone, because I loved her. The only difficulty was going to be in managing the virtually impossible situation that any combination of the three of us produced.

I reached the edge of the cliff in time to see a Mercedes staff car appear over the rise some fifty yards away and halt beside the field car. Steiner was still twenty or thirty feet below me and I ducked back out of sight and slid down to join him.

I had threaded the chain of my leg irons through my belt and I unbuckled it quickly. 'Get these on me sharp,' I ordered savagely. 'Radl's just arrived up top. You'd better be ready to give the performance of a lifetime.'

We got the leg irons on between us in seconds and he locked them hurriedly. I got to my feet and had barely started to climb when Radl appeared at the edge of the cliff. He had his usual guard of a couple of S.S. paratroopers with him and Schellenberg, who was looking distinctly worried.

'Morning, Radl,' I called cheerfully.

He ignored me and said to Steiner. 'What is the meaning of this? I arrive to check the road gang's progress and find Colonel Morgan absent in your charge.'

'By God, but it's a pull up that path in these damned irons,' I observed.

Radl ignored me again and Steiner said calmly, 'That's right, sir, I did have the requisite chit signed by Captain Schellenberg.'

Schellenberg was a thin-faced, middle-aged, greying man who wore steel-rimmed spectacles and looked as if he might have been an office manager before the war. I could imagine him standing at his desk in fear and trembling whenever Steiner's father visited the factory. He couldn't possibly have looked more worried then than he did now.

'Sergeant-Major Steiner did assure me, sir, that he needed Colonel Morgan's local knowledge.' He swallowed hard, perhaps appreciating for the first time how thin the story sounded. 'Some question of the beach defences.'

'The trouble is, sir,' Steiner said cheerfully, 'that the exceptionally strong current in the bay when the Mill-Race is running, has virtually scoured the beach clear of mines over the years, but they must be down there somewhere. Now we've got the spring storms due which isn't going to help.'

'It's a question of knowing where the current runs,' I put in helpfully. 'It curves into the beach and out again with quite exceptional force. When I was a boy we used to find a great bank of oysters under the headland there at low tide. My guess is you'll find more mines than oysters over there now.'

'Aiding the enemy, Colonel Morgan?' he said. 'Strange conduct for a British officer.'

'On the contrary. I agreed to advise Steiner on this problem on humanitarian grounds. The war, in case you hadn't noticed, Colonel Radl, is about to fall flat on its face. Those mines will be everyone's problem soon.'

There was an ominous silence and for a few moments it all hung in the balance. And when he accepted our explanation I couldn't quite believe it, for he knew we were lying and that the truth was something else again. I believe now that he had some dark purpose of his own, aimed not at me, but at Steiner.

'Very commendable of you, Colonel Morgan.' He nodded and said to Steiner. 'If your task here is finished, you will return the colonel to the road gang.' He started to move away followed by the others, paused and turned to me. 'They were having their meal break when we were up there, Colonel. I'm afraid you'll be out of luck.'

Now that struck him as funny. He was actually laughing as he got into the back of the Mercedes and was driven away.

Steiner said softly. 'He's beginning to really worry me, that one.'

'What's his game?' I asked him. 'He didn't believe us for a moment.'

'It's me,' Steiner said. 'He wants me broken on the wheel. Something special, you see. Only the best will do.'

'Is he going to get what he wants?'

And when he smiled, he suddenly looked about as dangerous as any man could. 'That will be the day, Owen Morgan,' he said softly. 'That indeed will be the day.'

His hand came out of his pocket holding my knife. He sprang the blade, examined it for a moment, then flicked it into the ground at my feet. I picked it up. 'Are you sure you want me to have this? When it comes right down to it, there could be a time when I might want to use it.'

He didn't seem to hear me, but shivered and looked up at the sky. 'The weather is going to break soon. I can feel it in my bones.'

'Those spring storms you mentioned to Radl?' I asked with a grin.

But he wasn't smiling. A small wind stirred the grass and I was suddenly cold—cold all the way through. He turned and walked away without a word and I followed him.

10 The Hand of God

Looking back on it all now, I don't think it would be fair to say that Fitzgerald hated or even disliked me. I think the truth of the matter was more complex than that. To put it in simple terms, he just didn't understand me. My background, my attitude to life, to the war, to what was going on about me, was something completely alien to his own highly personal view of things. There was no common point—not one on which we could meet.

Which was a pity from my point of view because he

seemed as a matter of deliberate policy, to grow more frigidly polite each day. I think he probably looked upon it as part of his martyrdom, trapped as he was in a world he did not understand, and never once in conversation failed to call me sir and always deferred to my judgement in even the most unimportant of situations. Naturally Sergeant Hagen and Wallace, while not understanding what was going on, took their cue from him, which didn't help!

Where Grant was concerned it was a lot less complex. He hated me for the humiliation of his defeat at our first meeting still rankled and in any case, he seemed to have a genuine contempt for small men which I have often noted in his kind.

The situation wasn't helped by the fact that during the days that followed, we worked on several occasions with Steiner and his Brandenbergers. He usually took the opportunity of speaking privately to me and I think Fitzgerald viewed this with something like suspicion. No, perhaps I was doing him an injustice to think that. It would probably be closer to the truth to say that he disapproved. The business on the jetty with the Brandenbergers had been an impulse of the moment that on reflection, he probably regretted although I suspect that Radl was completely to blame for this. The way he handled the business at the harbour, his blackmail over the Todt workers, had genuinely sickened Fitzgerald, so alien was it to his own nature and view of things.

Possibly his attitude to me was really a kind of withdrawal from the whole unpalatable situation, for none of this was war as he understood it. For the first time he had caught a glimpse of darker vistas and had retreated. He just didn't want to know. I think this explains why he so superbly came to life again to meet the challenge, the really worthwhile challenge of subsequent events.

One thing which became increasingly obvious to me was Steiner's quite unique position among the German garrison, men and officers alike. With some—and possibly this was true more of the officers—his step-father's name had its usual magic effect, but not so with the other ranks. With them, it was the sheer personality of the man, the legendary bravery, the inimitable touches like the silk scarf he always wore knotted at the neck to cover his Knight's Cross.

And when I talked in German with the Pioneers, with

Sergeant Braun and Schmidt who brought me gifts of terrible French cigarettes from Ezra, I realised there were
other considerations. These men had seen the Nigger project in operation, had seen Steiner and his men venture
out again and again on their incredible home-made underwater chariots. Had seen the group dwindle in number
day-by-day. Courage, after all, never goes out of fashion.

Perhaps it was this obvious adulation that Radl found
too hard to take or perhaps he simply didn't like him. On
the other hand, it was always possible that Steiner offended his sense of order. Of what was proper. He should
have been an officer and had set his face against it. He
was a gentleman who had preferred to serve in the ranks.
No sergeant-major on earth had the right to be what
Steiner was.

When we were working with Steiner and his men, Radl
appeared on more than one occasion in his Mercedes staff
car with bodyguard of S.S. bully boys armed to the teeth.
He usually called for Steiner and questioned what was
going on and always, one could sense the tension beneath
the surface of conventional military courtesies.

Things really came to a head for the whole world to see
on the first day of May. None of us knew then how close
the war was to its end, although some knowledge of how
things were shaping in Europe was getting through to almost everyone and not only by way of Ezra Scully's ille-
gal radio. The German signals personnel in the communi-
cations unit next door to the Platzkommandantur in Charlottestown, were just as much to blame, although at that
stage in the war, for a soldier to be caught listening to the
B.B.C. and passing on its news, could well mean execution.

But on St Pierre, things still ran their course, fortifications were still built, mines laid as elsewhere in the Channel Islands for the Commander-in-Chief showed every intention of carrying on the struggle long after the war in
Europe was finished.

As I have said, on the first day of May, a Tuesday, as I
remember, we were taken down to Granville and put to
work below the life-boat station. About twenty Todt
workers were already there when we arrived and Steiner
and his Brandenbergers came shortly afterwards. The area
below the boat-house, including the slipway, had been
bombed as Ezra had told me that first night and our task

was to clear a level sight for an extra blockhouse to be constructed.

The Brandenbergers were at work on the other side of the barbed wire laying additional mines although the beach was apparently already a death trap which didn't surprise me, for it was one of the few on the island where vehicles could conceivably have driven ashore from landing craft.

It was one of the Todt workers who raised the alarm first with a sudden cry and I glanced up to see a man in the water a hundred yards out, drifting helplessly in an inflatable life-jacket. The tide was beginning to run at four to five knots and he had obviously been swept in around the point. The odds were that the current would take him out again at the other end of the bay and something had to be done quickly. It was impossible to do anything from Granville because of the beach defences and then Ezra emerged from his cottage to see what all the fuss was about.

He took in the situation at a glance and said to Steiner. 'Best get the pilot boat out to him from Charlottestown, but I'll need help. A couple of your lads to take me in the field car and crew for me.'

Steiner called Sergeant Lanz and Schreiber over, but before he could give them their instructions, the Mercedes staff car appeared in the narrow street and braked to a halt beside the boathouse.

Radl came forward and looked out at the unfortunate wretch in the bay. 'Who is he?'

'I'm not sure,' Steiner told him. 'Probably an airman. He seems to be wearing a flying jacket. I'm sending Lanz and Schreiber with Mr Scully to get the pilot boat out.'

'I really despair of you at times, Steiner.' Radl sighed. 'How often have I told you that my jurisdiction does not extend beyond the mouth of the harbour? Anything that happens outside the breakwater is Navy business.'

He was legally correct, but such an incredible attitude could not just be put down to the kind of military mind that could only act according to the book. I don't think he was even being particularly bloody-minded. He was getting at Steiner again, that was the truth of it, trying to prod him into action—the wrong kind of action.

Steiner said quietly, 'I would respectfully remind the Colonel that the Nigger project comes under the direct control of Navy Group West.'

'My dear Steiner. The Nigger project no longer exists. You and your men are soldiers again. That argument won't wash at all.'

There was a nasty silence. No one spoke—no one at all and I heard Hagen whisper to Fitzgerald, 'For Christ's sake, sir, what goes on here? Isn't anyone going to do something for that poor guy?'

Fitzgerald ignored him and moved to join me. His face was pale, the eyes fixed rather wildly. He was obviously deeply distressed. 'Can't you do something? You seem to have influence around here most of the time.'

Which was the first remark of that kind he had made to me. 'What would you suggest?' I demanded.

I think he hated me at the moment. For a second, I thought he was going to strike me, but the fist and the boot were never his weapons. Instead, he turned and lurched towards Radl, almost losing his balance as he misjudged the length of his stride, and the chain tautened.

'Colonel Radl,' he said clearly in German, 'I must warn you, sir, that I have every intention of reporting your conduct in this matter to the proper authority at the first opportunity.'

Radl ignored him, moved past as if he didn't exist. He took out his cigarette case, selected one with care, placed it between his lips and glanced at Steiner. Steiner produced an old lighter he habitually used, a thing made from a rifle cartridge case and gave him a light.

'Thank you, Steiner.'

There was no sound, only the wind through the wire, and the clouds coming in fast from the horizon were grey and swollen with rain. The man in the water was moving fast, caught in the tidal current that swept him towards the far side of the bay. Quite suddenly, he seemed to change direction. He started to move in towards the shore in a great curve.

Someone cried out sharply, one of the Todt workers I think and then everyone seemed to hold their breath at the same moment. There was no surf worth speaking about. He simply floated in on the current and grounded about fifty yards below us.

He was an airman, Steiner had been right about that, in flying boots and sheepskin jacket. He lay face down in the shallows and then rolled over on his back.

'There you are, Steiner, the hand of God. Now he is indeed the Army's problem,' Radl said.

Problem was the right word, for the forty or fifty yards of white sand on the other side of the wire were a death trap and I was reminded of that cold dawn on Horseshoe.

'What are the Colonel's orders?' Steiner asked.

'My dear Steiner,' Radl's eyebrows arched in surprise. 'Surely this sort of thing is your specialty? I wouldn't dream of advising you.' He shrugged. 'Of course, I could not condone any breach of the defensive system such as took place at Horseshoe. You do understand?'

'Perfectly.' Steiner brought his heels together. 'With the Colonel's permission?'

Radl gave him a half salute and Steiner went to his four comrades who stood together in a small group. He spoke to them and they immediately started to enlarge the way through the wire they had been using earlier. Steiner turned and crossed to me and Ezra.

'Not like Horseshoe, Owen. Getting through the wire is easy here. It is the beach itself which is the problem.'

'He wants your hide, Manfred,' Ezra said urgently in a low voice. 'Don't give it to him.'

Steiner smiled, that strange, rather ironic smile of his. 'I have to win or lose on his terms, Ezra, don't you see that?' He looked at me. 'You understand, Owen?'

I nodded. 'What do you want me to do?'

'If I die, see that he does. Can I ask that much of you?'

'And more,' I said. 'By my own hand at close quarters, I promise you.'

'You will give Simone my love.'

It was a statement, not a request. He swung on heel and went down to the wire. They were almost through. Lanz clipped the last section and rolled it back. A twenty foot passage some three feet wide now gave clear access to the beach.

But what was he going to do? That was the question that everyone must have been asking. When the action came, it was so utterly incredible that for a brief moment, that uncanny silence continued.

Steiner lit a cigarette, took a couple of deep puffs, flicked it away, then walked through the wire to the beach as calmly as if he had been taking a stroll in the park on a Sunday afternoon. There was an involuntary gasp of horror and cries of dismay in several languages and then, as if by common consent, complete silence again.

He walked steadily across the beach without faltering and Ezra clutched at my arm and groaned. 'It's impossible, Owen. It would need a miracle.'

'No, just a hell of a lot of luck,' I said.

And he would get it, for once again, my flesh seemed to crawl and I felt suddenly cold and knew out of some strange foreknowledge, that he would survive. We all would for the moment, because there was a bigger game to be played.

After that, there wasn't a sound from anyone as we watched his back all the way down to the water. He reached the airman and dropped to one knee beside him. There was a kind of dry sob behind and I turned to see Hagen cross himself, his face shining with sweat.

'I'd keep holding on to my breath if I were you, laddie,' Grant told him. 'He's got to come back again.'

Steiner had the airman across his shoulders now in a fireman's lift and turned to face us. At that distance I could not see his expression and yet it was as if I could. I glanced at Radl who waited, a slight smile on his mouth and then I shuffled forward to the edge of the wire and cupped my hands.

'Come on, Manfred!' I called in English. 'You've drawn a Royal Flush.'

He started to walk, slowly because of the weight, his feet sinking deeply into the soft sand. Behind me, the crowd flooded forward, soldiers, Todt workers, Rangers and Brandenbergers, all mixed in together. There was not silence now, but a low murmur.

I heard the sound of a vehicle somewhere, but didn't take my eyes off Steiner. There was a movement in the crowd and Paddy Riley said from behind, 'Holy Mother of God.'

And then Simone was beside me, clutching my arm, her face white. 'Someone phoned the hospital from the battery,' she said, 'we came in the ambulance.'

'Let them through, damn you!' Riley cried in his terrible German and the crowd parted for a couple of medical orderlies with a stretcher.

Steiner was only fifteen or twenty yards away. He paused suddenly, his face wiped clear of all expression, right foot poised which wasn't surprising, for as the soft sand crumbled away, we saw that his foot rested on top of a mine. There was a terrified cry from someone in the crowd and then panic with men turning away in horror, some flinging themselves to the ground to avoid the blast of the explosion all expected.

It didn't come. Steiner stayed there, delicately balanced, intense concentration on his face and I pushed Simone away and went through the wire, my chain rattling like Marley's ghost.

When I got close enough, he smiled. 'What kept you?'

I got down on my knees, always a difficult manoeuvre because of the chain and gently scraped the sand away from the sides of the mine. Then I picked it up and put it down carefully to one side.

'You cold-blooded bastard,' he said.

I shook my head. 'Not particularly. I'd like to continue to live, but I can accept that I'm going to die. But not now, not here. There's something else, something coming, God knows what.'

Grey clouds spilled rain in a few heavy drops and I got up and led the way in through the wire to a roar from the crowd that must have been heard in Charlottestown. They parted to give us room and Steiner passed the airman over to the two orderlies. He was still unconscious, a boy of nineteen or twenty with three or four ragged bullet holes through one leg and plenty of blood on view.

Riley shouted for them to clear the way and went through the crowd in front of the stretcher shoving anyone who got in his way ruthlessly to one side. Simone put a hand on Steiner's arm looking as if she might burst into tears at any moment.

'I know,' he told her gently, 'but not now. Dr Riley needs you. Later, perhaps, you could let us know how the boy is?'

She went then, lost in the crowd that surged around Steiner. I was forgotten, which was as it should be for it had been his show. The S.S. Paratroopers cleared a way through and Steiner went forward to Radl who was standing by the Mercedes.

'Who was he, Steiner?' Radl asked.

'One of ours, sir, a naval reconnaissance pilot from one of the Brittany ports.'

'My congratulations. Naturally I shall submit an appropriate report.' He smiled. 'Who knows, perhaps another medal, eh?'

Again, I could not see Steiner's face and yet I knew beyond any shadow of a doubt that he was closer then than he had ever been to assaulting Radl physically. Somehow, he managed to restrain the impulse. Radl nodded to his driver, got into the Mercedes with his men and was driven away.

I suddenly felt rather tired, turned and found Fitzgerald at my shoulder. There was a strange, puzzled expression in his eyes. Poor devil, I was completely beyond his range of understanding.

'I can't make you out,' he said. 'Do you know that? Can't make you out at all.'

'Which makes two of us,' I commented sourly and shuffled away as the rain started to increase.

The crowd was breaking, Todt workers and soldiers returning to their labours, but something seemed to be happening. There was a buzz of conversation, men running from one group to another, soldiers and workers together again. There was actually laughter, a ragged cheer and then Ezra appeared, running through the crowd.

When he reached me, he seemed bereft of speech and I grabbed his arm to steady him. 'What is it, Ezra, what's gone wrong?'

'Gone wrong?' His head went back and his laughter lifted into the sky. 'God Almighty, wrong, he says.' When he looked at me again, his eyes were wet. 'The B.B.C. have broadcast a special message, Owen. They say the Russians are into Berlin. They say Hitler is dead.'

Beyond him, I saw Steiner staring across at me. Behind him, men were singing, weeping, laughing, embracing each other.

Ezra grabbed my arms. 'It's true, Owen, the bloody war is over, don't you see?'

But it wasn't—not for us. I knew it and Steiner knew it. Thunder rumbled somewhere above in those grey clouds and then they spilt wide open and it really started to rain.

11   Rough Justice

After the shock of that first report of what was thought to have taken place in Berlin, no one was really in the mood to carry on with work on the beach at Granville. The Todt workers spent most of the time arguing among themselves, for now that the first ecstatic response had faded, some found the news impossible to believe. Braun and Schmidt, the two Pioneer sergeants who were supposed to be in charge of things obviously didn't have the heart to do anything about it and most of the German troops present seemed to be completely dazed by the turn events had taken.

Fitzgerald had been speaking to his men hurriedly in a low voice and now he shuffled over to me. 'What do you think? Could it be true?'

'I don't see why not. Ezra heard it with his own ears, didn't he?'

'Then it's only a matter of time. They're all through. We made it.'

'Now *that* remains to be seen,' I said.

He frowned instantly, but was prevented from saying anything further by the arrival of Braun who had been in conference with Schmidt and Steiner. Obviously, some plan of action had been agreed.

'If you would be good enough to call your men, Colonel,' he told me politely, 'We have decided to march everyone back to Charlottestown. You can wait in the church with the Todt workers until we can discover exactly what is happening.'

The parish church of St Pierre stood in a large cemetery behind high walls half-way up the main street by the Platzkommandantur. It had been stripped of its pews early in the war and for a while had been used as a food store. For the past year it had housed Todt workers who could have done worse, for the main fabric was Norman and the walls were three feet thick which at least kept out the worst excesses of the winter storms.

As I say, the pews had been long since removed and the Todt workers slept on the floor. The area beyond the altar rail still seemed to have been kept intact. The choir stalls were as I always remembered them and the altar itself had not been violated although the altar cloth and candlesticks had been taken away.

When we arrived, no one seemed to know what to do and I don't suppose the little church had seen such a crowd since high holy days before the war. The rain was falling so heavily now that everyone crowded in, soldiers

as well as Todt workers and prisoners and Steiner and the
Pioneer sergeants got together again in a corner to discuss
the situation. Finally, he left with Sergeant Schmidt and
Braun came over looking strangely awkward. 'Sergeant-
Major Steiner has gone to see Colonel Radl.' He shrugged
helplessly. 'To be frank with you, Colonel, no one really
knows what to do.'

'So we wait?'

He gave me a wry smile. 'We have been doing that for
some time, is it not so? Please God I may see my
Gretchen again now. Something I had not felt able to
count on.'

He returned to his men and I lit one of my French cigarettes and pushed my way through the crowd to the side
door which was not guarded, an oversight on Braun's part
which I could well understand considering the circumstances.

It was raining so heavily that it was not possible to see
the wall on the north side of the cemetery. My father's
grave was up there by a large cypress tree and my mother
had been laid to rest beside him. I could see that tree
now, standing straight in the rushing rain, a dark sentinel.

Behind me there was laughter, voices in argument, a
dangerous excitement. It had been a mistake to bring everyone back together like this. The voice of reason was
not the voice of the crowd, and men who had been
treated like most of those who now crammed the church
could not be counted on to act with reason in such circumstances.

The door opened behind me and Hagen appeared.
'We've been looking all over for you, sir. Miss de Beaumarchais is here. She wants a word with you.'

I went back in with him and pushed my way through
the noisy throng. Simone was by the main entrance with
Sergeant Braun and Fitzgerald and his Rangers. She
looked pale and excited, an unnatural flush to her cheeks.

She caught my sleeve. 'Isn't it incredible, Owen? The
hospital is in an uproar.'

The noise level by now had reached such proportions
that it was difficult to hear oneself speak. I told Braun we
would go into the porch and he nodded to the Pioneer
who stood on duty at the door, a machine pistol slung
negligently from his shoulder. The door closed behind us
and for the moment, we were alone, rain drifting in,

splashing in great drops on the cold stone flags.

'Is it true?' she demanded. 'Can it really be so after all
these years?'

'Everything comes to an end sooner or later,' I told her.
'Good or bad. One of Nature's more infallible laws.'

The headscarf and old trenchcoat she wore were soaked
with rain, but she was beyond caring about such triviali-
ties. 'I really came to tell you about the young pilot. He's
going to be fine. Paddy thought the leg might have to go
when he first saw him, but now he seems to think there's
every chance of a good recovery.'

Which added something to the day. 'Whoever he is,
he'll certainly have a tale to tell his grandchildren.'

She nodded in a strange, abstracted way and stared out
into the rain. 'Perhaps we all will, but I have a feeling.
Oh, it's so difficult to put into words.'

'Radl?' I put an arm around her. 'Even the Radl's of this
world go down to defeat on occasion.'

'I suppose so.' When she looked up, her face was an-
guished. 'Dear God, I hope so. I must go now, Owen.
Paddy needs me at the hospital. Tell Manfred.'

She did not kiss me and that, I think, was significant.
She turned and ran into the rain, taking the path round
the side of the church that led through the cemetery to
the back gate.

For some reason, I felt rather sad. I went back inside
the church. The noise was more deafening than ever and
to add to it, someone was playing the organ. Sergeant
Obermeyer, lost in a world of his own devising playing
Bach again and I wondered how long it had been for him.

Fitzgerald was in a corner with his men and Braun who
looked worried and helpless. When I approached, Fitzgerald said grimly, 'This whole thing is getting out of hand if
you ask me.'

'Not for long if I know my Radl. I give it another five
minutes. I'd keep out of the line of fire if I were you.'

I pushed my way through the crowd, ignoring the slaps
on the back from the Todt workers and made for the side
door again, the door poor Braun had failed to have
guarded. Outside, the rain was falling as heavily as ever, a
solid curtain that from the force of it, seemed intent on
drowning the whole world.

I could see the cypress tree standing straight up there
by the boundary wall beside my father's grave and on im-

pulse, stepped out into the rain and followed the gravel
path between the tombstones.

The scream seemed to come from another world, I
paused, my head turned, unsure of the direction. It came
again, the cry of a woman in fear for her life. That
damned chain. I forgot it as usual, tried to run and fell
flat on my face. I picked myself up and Simone ran out of
the murk towards me.

Her coat had been torn from her back, and the old cot-
ton dress she wore underneath was in shreds, her shoulder
and one breast bare. The man who pursued her was one
of the Todt workers, a Pole I had noticed on the road
gang mainly because of his great size.

It was understandable, for no man on the island had
access to any kind of a woman for God knows how
long, and for the past six months, Simone had been the
only one on view. I had seen the way men looked as she
passed. Had not liked it, but had at least understood. Presumably he had been in the porch at the side entrance,
had seen her take the short cut through the cemetery and
had followed.

She got to me, arms reaching out, sobbing hysterically
and I barely had time to shove her out of the way as he
arrived. By then, of course, he had long since passed the
point of being able to make any rational judgement, which
wasn't surprising in the circumstances. There wasn't much
I could do considering that damned chain. I ducked, hit
him as hard as I could in the guts and we went down together, rolling over and over, fetching up against a tomb-
stone.

Unfortunately for me, he was on top and his hands fastened around my throat in a grip like iron. Things became
even darker. I had secreted my knife, for obvious reasons,
in a crude pocket I had made inside my waistband at the
rear and I couldn't get at it. I concentrated on his little
fingers, twisting them outwards so that he screamed in
pain. For a while, his stinking breath alone seemed close
to suffocating me and then, as I increased the pressure on
the fingers, he screamed again and released his grip.

My hand went back to strike hard across his throat.
There was no need. Steiner was there, his face white in
the rain, an expression on it like the wrath of God. He
dragged the Pole backwards, spun him round and slammed
his clenched fist into the face again and again and yet

again, holding him with his left hand, hammering him into the ground.

I lay there, still choking, struggling for breath and Fitzgerald and Grant appeared and lifted me up between them. To say that the situation had changed would have been an understatement. Radl stood a couple of yards away, twenty or so S.S. paratroopers fanned out behind him.

The Pole was on his knees now, Radl made a sign and two of his men ran forward, took him from Steiner and dragged him back to Radl. Radl looked down at him, genuine loathing on his face and I was reminded again of my first estimate of him. Some Roundhead fanatic, capable of anything.

He kicked the Pole in the body. 'I will teach you manners, you animal. Take him inside.'

They dragged the poor wretch away and Radl unbuttoned his greatcoat, crossed to Steiner who stood holding Simone and draped the coat over her shoulders.

'That this should have happened under my command is unforgivable.' She seemed incapable of any kind of rational response and I think he realised as much. 'My car is at the gate, Steiner. You will take Miss de Beaumarchais to the hospital.'

Steiner picked her up in his arms and went. Radl turned to me, 'And now, Colonel Morgan, if you and your friends would be so good as to follow me, you shall see a little justice administered!'

Which didn't sound good, but even I wasn't prepared for what happened. Inside the church the Todt workers were crouched in against the wall. The Brandenbergers and a few Pioneers were drawn up by the door and the S.S. boys covered everyone with their usual efficiency.

Two of them held the Pole between them. His face was covered with blood from Steiner's beating and he seemed dazed as if not understanding what was happening. Sergeant Braun stood between another two, his hands tied behind his back.

There was complete silence as Radl walked slowly to the middle of the church and looked the Todt workers over. His voice, when he spoke, was surprisingly mild.

'You have been extremely foolish, all of you. You believed a lie. A stupid and senseless piece of propaganda put out by the enemy with the sole purpose of causing the

kind of behaviour we have seen here today. A lie, because
the announcement has no basis in fact. The Fuhrer lives,
there is no question of defeat, the German army still
fights.' His voice began to rise a little. 'I have been in
touch with our headquarters in Guernsey and can assure
you that whatever happens in Europe, we will continue to
fight in the Channel Islands. Do you hear me? We will
continue the fight!'

His voice echoed in the rafters and up there, pigeons
lifted in alarm. 'There will be no breakdown of law and
order on St Pierre while I command, no slackening of discipline for anyone and in that, I include my own troops.'

By this time the Todt workers were back to what they
had been before: broken, beaten animals without hope who
existed, took what came and expected only the worst.

Radl snapped his fingers and the Pole was dragged forward. 'We have here an excuse for a man, a walking animal who has behaved like the beast he is. Very well, he
shall be treated accordingly.'

They slung a rope up across a rafter and knotted it
around the Pole's throat. He stood there staring dumbly
from face to face, completely unaware of what was about
to happen.

When they brought Braun forward, they had to half
carry him as he seemed near to collapse. Radl stood looking at him for a long moment, and when he spoke, his
voice was cold and hard.

'What happened here was your fault, Braun. You were
in charge and yet allowed yourself to be affected by this
foul rumour as much as anyone here. The attack on Miss
de Beaumarchais could not have taken place had you
remembered to place a guard on the side door. You are a
disgrace to your uniform, a disgrace to the German army.'

Braun tried to speak, but started to sob instead and another rope was tossed over the rafter, one end knotted
crudely about his neck.

They hanged them both by the simple expedient of
hauling them six feet off the ground, three S.S. to each
rope. They took several of the longest minutes of my life
to go and it was anything but pleasant to watch.

There was the odd gasp here and there and someone
started to sob hysterically, but otherwise there was little
reaction. Radl was firmly back in control. The Todt workers at least knew when they were beaten.

Radl waited till all movement had ended, then turned and nodded to one of the S.S. sergeants. 'You may return the prisoners to their quarters in Fort Edward.'

We went out through the main door and lined up in the rain. Fitzgerald seemed to have aged some more and the others were like different men, all of them, for I think that for the first time, the possibility of the same kind of summary execution had assumed reality for them.

The sergeant ordered us away, but as we started to march, Radl called from the porch, 'A moment. Something I was forgetting.'

As he came out into the rain, he was smiling so I knew it had to be bad, whatever it was.

'Good news, Colonel. A signal from St Denis was handed to me as I was leaving my house. The *Pride of Hamburg* took advantage of the bad weather to leave harbour an hour ago.'

'With Olbricht on board?' I said.

'Naturally. With luck she should be here by noon tomorrow.'

He walked away through the rain, humming to himself cheerfully.

12 Storm Warning

He was a good soldier, Radl, I'll give him that. As we were marched off through the rain to Fort Edward, he returned to his headquarters and started to set his house in order. The small garrison was deployed around the island defences and every bunker, every gun emplacement, was fully manned and ready for action. This meant, of necessity, that in Charlottestown itself, he could keep no more than thirty or forty troops, but this seemed justified at the time and they were mainly S.S. paratroopers from his old regiment, the men General Muller had brought with him originally.

As for the Rangers, the storm burst when we were back inside the old ammunition store at Fort Edward. Sergeant Hagen, who was inclined to be emotional at the best of times, cracked wide open.

'We're going to die, all of us. All that guy has to do is

raise an eyebrow and his men will give us what those two poor bastards at the church got without thinking twice about it.' He appealed to me wildly. 'Ain't it the truth, Colonel? Go on, you tell 'em. You know these devils better than any of us.'

'That's enough, laddie,' Grant told him sharply. 'That kind of talk won't get us anywhere, will it, sir?'

He turned to Fitzgerald, but Fitzgerald didn't seem to hear him. He sat on a bench, staring listlessly into space, fingers intertwining ceaselessly.

Grant spoke to me with obvious reluctance. 'I don't think he's feeling too well, poor lad.'

I think it was then that I first appreciated his genuine fondness for Fitzgerald. 'I'm not surprised,' I said. 'Who is?'

'What do we do now, sir?'

'What can we do?' I shrugged. 'I never did have as much faith in Radl as the rest of you. I've seen his kind in action before. Escape, if that's on your mind, is out of the question now. Those are S.S. paratroopers outside, not Pioneers.'

'What do we do?' Hagen demanded wildly.

'Pray,' I said. 'Hope and pray. And then you could always follow my example and get some sleep.'

But I doubt if any of us got much sleep that night. The rain drummed against the roof ceaselessly and from midnight on, the wind started to moan. Up there on the battlements I could hear the sea pounding in across the rocks.

I lay wrapped in a damp blanket, and listened to it as it got worse. Steiner had been right in his prophecy. Spring storms could be bad in these waters. As bad as anything winter could provide. The *Pride of Hamburg* must be having a rough passage, but then, as Steiner had said, Ritter, her captain, preferred dirty weather.

Everything could happen exactly as Radl had predicted. The *Pride of Hamburg* couldn't help but evade the Royal Navy on such a night. She would sail into Charlottestown harbour at noon and tie up at the north landing stage. Korvettenkapitan Karl Olbricht would be piped ashore or whatever they did, with full honours to take over his new post. And as his first task he would be presented with the problem of Owen Morgan and his happy band.

But what if Olbricht didn't fancy the idea? What if he was the old-fashioned kind? Navy men usually were. What was the wording of Paragraph Six of the Kommandobefehl again? *In the case of non-compliance with this order, I shall bring to trial before a court martial, any commander or other officer who has failed to carry out his duty or who has acted contrary to it.*

But the Kommandobefehl had been a personal order from the Fuhrer himself who was now dead according to the B.B.C. which at this stage in the game should be enough to make any sensible man think twice in such a situation. But if Olbricht decided against the executions, how would Radl react? *Radl.* Always one had to come back to Radl.

I finally did get off to sleep, but woke just after dawn to find that the wind was worse than ever. The sea was a heaving carpet of broken water and whitecaps that faded into the heavy rain.

At six-thirty, the door opened and young Durst, the boy soldier, came in with a pail of coffee, black bread and cold sausages. The coffee was ersatz, but hot. Fitzgerald was the only one who didn't bother getting up and Grant filled an enamel mug and took it to him.

I smiled at Durst. 'How are things in the outside world?'

'Bad, very bad.' He shook his head. 'They say the weather will continue to worsen. They managed to get the met. forecast from Guernsey before the weather interfered with the reception. I heard a couple of signalmen discussing it at the cookhouse.'

An S.S. sergeant appeared in the doorway and called to him roughly and he left in a hurry. As the door was bolted, I gave the others a translation and Hagen's eyes came to life again.

'Mabey that damned boat won't get here after all.'

'You could be right,' I said. 'Anything can happen in these waters once the weather starts turning dirty.'

I left him discussing the prospect enthusiastically with Corporal Wallace and climbed up to one of the old gun ports. Down in the harbour on my left, the sea was coming in over the breakwater in enormous white curtains of spray and some of the fishing boats were already adrift from their moorings.

The view seaward was fantastic. Leaden clouds belched

heavy rain, dropping to meet waves that were now really beginning to lift. Through a sudden break in the curtain, I caught a glimpse of the Pinnacles half a mile out standing grimly above a welter of white water.

The door opened and the S.S. sergeant appeared and ordered us out. Fitzgerald sat on the bench, nursing a mug of coffee in both hands, staring into space. His face was grey and haggard and I don't think I've ever seen such a change in a man.

He got to his feet reluctantly and followed the rest of us out. Sergeant Lanz waited beside a truck in the court-yard, his black oilskins streaming moisture.

'Radl putting us to work again?' I asked.

He nodded. 'Things are pretty chaotic at the harbour. Sergeant-Major Steiner is down there now.'

At least it was better than sitting around in the ammunition store, listening to the howl of the wind and waiting for something to happen. We climbed into the back of the truck followed by the S.S. sergeant and a couple of his men and were driven away.

Charlottestown had always been a notoriously bad anchorage when strong easterly or north-easterly winds were blowing, for quite a sea was apt to build up inside the breakwater.

When we reached the harbour things, if anything, looked worse. There was a heavy swell inside the breakwater and the wind was gusting to Force 7 or 8 by my judgement. The harbour itself was in a hell of a state. At least half-a-dozen fishing boats were loose and the crowd on the jetty, mainly Todt workers and Pioneers, didn't seem to know what to do about it. Major Brandt and Schellenberg were standing at the edge of the harbour wall above the lower jetty.

The pilot boat was down there, a thirty-foot diesel launch with a high old-fashioned wheelhouse. Ezra was inside and the Brandenbergers were crewing for him. Steiner was at the bow to receive the line as someone cast off from the jetty. He wore black oilskins and his head was bare. He glanced up and saw me as I reached the edge and looked over. There was time for a wave, no more than that, before the bow line was cast off and Ezra took the old launch out into the harbour.

In that confined space and with the way the sea was

building up, securing the fishing boats was rather like
trying to tie down, one-by-one, a corral full of wild
horses. There was no certainty as to what would happen
next for with the shallow bottom in that part of the harbour the waves were apt to do unaccountable things and
squalls were frequent.

But Ezra had a genius for such things. He ran across
the bows of his first choice, spun the wheel over at the
very last moment and laid alongside for Steiner to vault
over the rail into the fishing boat, line in hand. He secured her quickly and Ezra turned to tow her in to the
jetty.

They tied her up with some difficulty and went back for
another. As I stood watching, a voice said, 'They are
sailors, those men. All of them. Soldiers perhaps, but good
sailors also.'

It was Warger, the harbourmaster in oilskins and
sou'wester. 'They've got the right man in charge and that's
what really makes the difference,' I said.

'Ezra?' He nodded in agreement. 'The best—the best
I've ever seen with small boats in a heavy sea, but this
. . .' He glanced up at the leaden sky. 'This is exceptional
for the time of year. This is not good—not good at all.'

'What's the forecast?'

'Unfortunately we have lost direct radio contact with
Guernsey.' He glanced furtively around to make sure no
one could overhear him. 'The B.B.C. have put out a gale
warning and the barometer in my office is falling fast—
very fast.'

'What about the wind speeds?'

'I have an anemometer fixed up on the roof of Fort
Windsor. I've sent an orderly up there to check and report regularly by field telephone.'

'You think it's going to get worse?'

'I think so. Force 10, maybe even 11 before she is
through. Don't you? You were raised in these waters.'

Force 10 or 11? *Full storm verging on hurricane conditions!* I'd known it bad, but never as bad as that—not at
this time of the year. And then I remembered a tale that
Ezra had once told me of the days when he was barely
seventeen and working as an inshore fisherman. A steel
hulled windjammer had gone hard on the Pinnacles, the
Barbary Queen out of Liverpool in ballast for Brest. The
end of April and a storm such as no man living could re-

call the equal of. They had a pulling life-boat in those days and had been unable to get beyond the breakwater, had smashed her oars like rotten sticks, had failed even with fresh oars and a double crew at the second attempt. The *Barbary Queen* had vanished by morning, might as well never have existed except for the bodies that came in with the tide for a week or more. But that was something special, Ezra used to say. The sort of thing that came along only once in a lifetime. But there was movement now and work to be done, the Pioneers shepherding the Todt workers along to the end of the jetty where the sea was coming in hard through a great gap left by the naval bombardment of the previous year. God knows why they hadn't done something about it before now, but I suppose it had taken a real storm to expose the weakness of the situation. Certainly with the kind of erosion that was taking place as the sea pounded in, it was definitely possible that a breach might be made all the way across that would separate one entire section of the jetty from the rest.

There was plenty of rubble to hand from the ruins of some of the old seventeenth century houses which had been demolished in the bombardment. Several lines were formed and stones and bricks were passed from hand-to-hand until they reached the seat of the trouble and were thrown into the great hole in the sea wall.

By chance, I found myself at that end. It was a wretched business, waves breaking in one after another without pause, cascading thirty feet into the air and showering us with icy water.

I was soon soaked to the skin and bitterly cold. There seemed no end to it. It was like one of those bad dreams in which one tries to fulfil an impossible task, for everything we threw into the breach disappeared without a trace.

After an hour or so more Todt workers arrived and we were pulled out of line to take a rest. A truck arrived and hot coffee was dispensed from buckets to everyone.

Fitzgerald sat in the lee of a ruined wall not far away, but didn't look in the mood for conversation. Grant and the others were standing in one of the coffee queues. At least they were dressed for the weather in their camouflaged waterproof smocks and trousers which was more than I was. My Guernsey was sodden, heavy with water, but there was little that I could do about that.

I found myself a corner that was at least protected from the wind and it was there that Warger discovered me. He had an old yellow oilskin in his hand and held it out to me. 'Please, Colonel, I could see you from my office. This is not good. It is barbaric.'

'For everyone here, not just me.' I pulled on the oilskin and buttoned it. 'My thanks.'

He glanced furtively around with the same expression as when he had spoken of the B.B.C. weather forecast and produced a half bottle of rum. 'I should not tell you this, but they have had word from the *Pride of Hamburg*.'

I coughed as the rum burned its way down. 'Trouble?'

'Bad trouble.' His face was grave. 'She is ten miles to the south-west and making heavy weather of it. Ritter says she had already sustained massive damage to her superstructure.'

'How's the wind now?'

'Gale force, but twice my man has recorded gusts of 90 knots an hour up there on the fort. Could the *Pride of Hamburg* get into harbour in such conditions?'

'He'll have to, won't he? Nowhere else for him to go.'

I took another pull at the rum bottle and Major Brandt appeared from the crowd, hesitated, then crossed towards us. There was no point in trying to hide the bottle, but he didn't seem to notice it.

'This is a bad business, Colonel,' he said. 'I am sorry to see you like this. You understand?'

'I'll do better than that, I'll drink to it,' I swallowed again. 'To hell with Colonel Radl.'

I held out the bottle, some sort of challenge, or perhaps it was the rum talking, but I think it was more than that. I liked him. He was a good man and I wanted him on my side if only in thought.

He nodded soberly and yet there was a glint in his eye! 'That is extremely kind of you,' The bottle was raised to his lips, his head went back. 'Excellent, Colonel Morgan, I congratulate you on your source of supply.' He handed the bottle back gravely. 'And now, Warger, we will inspect the breakwater. I am informed that the end is beginning to disappear into the sea.'

'An old story,' I said. 'Been happening for years.'

They went off together, heads bowed to the driving rain

and I walked over to where Fitzgerald squatted miserably against the wall, ignoring Grant who stood over him holding a mug of coffee.

I handed the rum bottle to the big Scot. 'There you are, you Highland bastard, get some of that into him and a drop over for yourself if you're careful.'

I turned away before he could say anything and went to the edge of the jetty. Ezra and the Brandenbergers had only two more to go now. I watched him circle another fishing boat, then swoop in suddenly. Someone jumped, missed his footing, but caught at a rail. There was a heart-stopping moment as Ezra fought to keep the pilot boat away from the dangling figure. No more than a couple of feet in it as he reversed his engines and pulled her away. But that, after all, was life . . .

The weather steadily deteriorated as the morning wore on and we continued to work desperately in shifts to fill the breach. It was hopeless. I suppose someone should have seen that from the beginning, but men can seldom see reason when faced with the elements, that is the strange thing.

By eleven o'clock, Ezra and the Brandenbergers had completed their task in the harbour and had tied up the pilot launch to the lower jetty. The swell in the harbour was quite something by then which hadn't made the job any easier.

I was resting again in the lee of my own particular wall when Warger found me. He crouched down, his face working. 'They've heard from the *Pride of Hamburg* again, Colonel.'

'Bad news?' A stupid question for I only had to look at his face for my answer.

'Engine trouble of some kind,' he told me hoarsely. 'In his last message, Ritter said he was having difficulty in keeping her head into the sea. He's lost most of his lifeboats and those that are left are damaged.'

'How far out?'

'A couple of miles, but now they've lost radio contact.'

I think I knew then what was going to happen—what must happen as so often in the past. But part of me rebelled for all sorts of reasons. Refused to believe that it would.

It was a moment or so later that someone gave a cry

and pointed and when I looked out to sea, there was the *Pride of Hamburg* a mile or so out. We all got the briefest of glimpses of her and then she disappeared.

The wind was getting stronger, I felt the physical impact of it so that when it gusted, I had to put my head down and lean hard into it to keep my footing.

Again the *Pride of Hamburg* lifted on the crest of a wave, then disappeared as suddenly. Disaster had its own smell and there was not a man there who failed to sense it then. All discipline was lost. There was a chorus of cries and everyone stopped working and moved to the harbour wall.

Ezra and Steiner came up from the lower jetty and joined Warger and myself. Strangely, it was to me that Ezra spoke and no one else, although it made sense when you thought of it, for we alone knew what was almost certain to happen.

'Did you see her, Owen?'

I nodded. 'Warger says she's got trouble in the engine room. Hardly making any headway.'

'God help all aboard if that's true. Only one end out there in weather like this.'

'The Pinnacles?' Steiner said.

I nodded. 'Unless you believe in miracles.'

A field car drove up, scattering the crowd and Brandt jumped out and joined us. 'Can you see her? I've been in touch with Colonel Radl. He's on his way down. They've lost radio contact completely.'

'How many men on board?' Steiner asked.

'Forty-eight including the crew.'

Everything else was forgotten except the tragedy that was being enacted out there in that cauldron where the sea was the only power worth considering. The Rangers had joined us and Fitzgerald, in some strange way seemed to have come to life again.

'Can't somebody do something?' he demanded.

'What would you suggest?'

'Isn't there a life-boat?'

'As a matter of fact, there is, only there are one or two snags. In the first place, it's sitting in the boathouse at Granville all ready for launching along a slipway that doesn't exist, on to a beach that's riddled with mines. On top of that, there's no crew unless you consider Ezra man enough on his own.'

Ezra looked at me sharply. 'There's yourself, Owen, don't forget that. The best second coxswain next to your Dad that I ever had.'

Which was all very nice, but hardly calculated to get us anywhere. I don't know why, but for a while, the wind seemed to clear the rain out there on the edge of nowhere and we saw the Pinnacles half a mile out, jagged black teeth rearing from a welter of white water.

I should say the *Pride of Hamburg* was no more than three hundred yards away from the reef at that point and drifting in fast. She fired a maroon and then another, though God knows what response she expected. It was round about then that Radl arrived in the Mercedes.

He stood on the harbour wall with a pair of field glasses and watched without saying anything. Finally, he lowered them and turned to the harbourmaster. 'Not good, Warger. What do you think will happen?'

'She'll strike, Colonel Radl,' I cut in. 'She'll run straight in on the Pinnacles. Can't avoid it now.'

'You think so?' He turned, raising the glasses again, and a couple of moments later, she did just that.

I have never seen such distress as I saw now on the faces of the men crowding the jetty. German soldiers, Todt workers, prisoners—everyone was affected. Strange how at the tail-end of a war whose casualties could be reckoned in millions, such anguish could be shown for forty-eight human beings faced with death in an impossible situation. But that is the way of the world and the sea, man's oldest enemy. All unite against it or die.

It was Fitzgerald who spoke first, coming finally to life again in the most uncanny manner. 'We've got to do something.'

Radl said sharply, 'Don't be stupid. In the first place such an operation would be outside the scope of my command and in any case, we haven't the facilities.' He shook his head and put his field glasses back in their case. 'They have their life-boats. They must do what they can to help themselves.'

'In that sea?' Fitzgerald demanded. 'Nothing could live in that—no boat could survive it.'

'Exactly,' Radl told him crisply. 'A realist like myself, I see, Major Fitzgerald.'

I had noticed Steiner and his Brandenbergers with their

heads together at the top of the steps and now he moved forward and stood to attention formally. 'With the Colonel's permission, I would like to make an attempt to reach the *Pride of Hamburg*. My men have all volunteered to go with me.'

'In what, may I ask?' Radl asked.

'The pilot boat.'

Even Ezra couldn't stand still for that one. 'What bloody nonsense are ye talking now, lad?' he demanded. 'You wouldn't even get outside the breakwater.'

'Thank you, Mr Scully,' Radl said. 'Commonsense is always refreshing.'

'I should still like permission to try,' Steiner persisted.

'Which I refuse to give you.'

There was silence, the wind scattered rain in our faces like ice-water. Surprisingly, it was Brandt who spoke next, hesitantly, it's true, but what he said, he said for all of us.

'But Colonel, men will die out there. True, to rescue them may be an impossible thing, but we must try, surely you see that?'

But that was exactly what Radl could not see. He frowned uncertainly, mystified by the new kind of animal Brandt had become. 'You would be willing to go with them in the pilot launch, Brandt?'

Brandt's face was grey. He looked out across the harbour through the blown spray and I knew that he was afraid. I don't know what happened inside him, but something did. When he turned to face Radl again, he was actually smiling slightly.

'I am the worst damned sailor you ever saw, Colonel, but yes . . . if Steiner thinks he could use me, then I go.'

Radl nodded slowly, then turned to Steiner. 'And could you, Steiner?'

There was more to the question than that, of course, much more. Steiner half-opened his mouth to speak, then glanced out to sea. An enormous squall raced across the harbour, tore a fishing boat from its moorings and proceeded to pound it to matchwood against the jetty. He didn't bother to reply. The pilot launch, even if it managed to defy Ezra's prophecy and get beyond the breakwater, could never last in such a sea.

'So, as everyone appears to have decided to act sensibly, we shall return to our work, shall we not? Good day, gentlemen.'

Radl saluted, turned and walked to his Mercedes. As it moved away, Fitzgerald said, 'Damn that bastard to hell, but he's right. There just isn't anything we can do, is there, Colonel Morgan?'

I don't know why he was appealing to me, but in any case, I didn't really hear what he was saying. I had something else entirely on my mind. A 41-foot, Watson-type motor life-boat named the *Owen Morgan.*

13 Mutiny

We drove into Charlottestown in Brandt's field car, those of us who were most concerned with the affair which meant Brandt, Steiner, Captain Schellenberg, Ezra, Fitzgerald and myself.

Radl was not at the Platzkommandantur, but at his house, the old rectory on the other side of the church from the main street. I had visited it often in childhood and it still looked much the same except for the two S.S. guards who stood outside the porch in the rain getting wet.

There was a large square hall inside with an Adam fireplace in which a fire of driftwood burned. There was a painting of my father's above it, a view of the Pinnacles in winter from Fort Edward.

Radl was apparently having an early lunch and was holding a napkin in one hand when he appeared from the dining room. He wasn't pleased. 'And what, may I ask, is the meaning of this?'

'With your permission, Colonel,' Brandt said, 'Colonel Morgan has an idea. A way of possibly helping those on the *Pride of Hamburg.*

'Indeed?' Radl turned to me slowly.

'It's really quite simple,' I said. 'There's a life-boat at Granville.'

'Named the *Owen Morgan,*' he cut in. 'A landed whale, Colonel Morgan. No slipway and if there was, a beach studded with mines.'

'We drag her overland to Charlottestown,' I said, 'And launch her in the harbour.'

He raised the napkin to his mouth. 'And for the crew?'

'I was a member of the crew here before the war when Ezra Scully was coxswain. Sergeant-Major Steiner and his men have all volunteered.'

'And so have mine, sir,' Fitzgerald put in.

Radl stared at him incredulously. 'Have they, indeed?'

'None of them have any life-boat experience,' I said, 'but it seemed to us that both by training and temperament, the Rangers and Brandenbergers are likely to make the best crew we're likely to find.'

Perhaps I had put it to him in the wrong way, for he seemed to lose his temper completely. 'Who the devil do you think you are, Morgan?' It was the first time he had failed to give me my rank. 'I am in command here and I say no to your crazy scheme. You understand?' He glared ferociously at each of us in turn. 'Now get out of here.'

He turned and Steiner said quietly, 'No, I don't really think that we can, Colonel Radl.'

He produced a Luger from one of his oilskin pockets and Schellenberg gave an involuntary gasp. All of us were taken by surprise and certainly no such action had been mooted when I had put my plan to them down at the harbour for the good and sufficient reason that no one had really considered the possibility that Radl might refuse.

'You see we don't have the time to argue any longer, Colonel Radl,' Steiner said. 'The *Pride of Hamburg* could hang on those rocks out there for the rest of the day. On the other hand, the sea could tear her off within the next couple of hours. I'm afraid that I must insist that you see our point of view.'

'So, at last we have it, Steiner. At last.' Radl was actually smiling, if smile you could call it. 'In the open in your true colours as you really are. No step-father to hide behind now—no medals. You'll kick on air like Braun before I'm through with you.'

I think it was that little speech which was the final nail in his own coffin for until then, I suspect that Brandt had been wavering, stunned by the enormity of it all. But now, he moved forward, hand out.

'Give it to me, Steiner.'

Steiner looked him full in the face for a long time then passed the Luger over, butt first. Brandt's next words wiped the triumphant smile from Radl's face. 'Sergeant-Major Steiner is acting under my orders, Colonel Radl. I am in command here now.'

'Are you mad, Brandt?' Radl demanded. 'On whose authority?'

'My own. I consider that you have failed to carry out your duties in a manner consistent with your responsibilities as a German officer. I therefore assume command as is my right and am prepared to defend such action before any necessary court martial. You will consider yourself under house arrest.'

Radl laughed wildly. 'And you think I will sit still and say nothing? This is mutiny.'

'If you do not, I will shoot you.' Brandt turned to the rest of us. 'We don't want any trouble at this stage, especially with the S.S., so it would be wiser to allow things to appear as normal as possible. I shall stay here with Colonel Radl. The sooner the rest of you get to work, the better. You, Schellenberg, will be nominally in charge, but I would suggest that you take any advice Mr Scully or Colonel Morgan are willing to offer you.'

'I warn you, Brandt, for the last time,' Radl said.

'And I warn you, Colonel Radl, any kind of a wrong move and I put a bullet into you. You will now oblige me by returning to the dining room.'

Radl threw his napkin on the floor and swung on heel. Brandt followed him and paused at the door, 'Good luck, gentlemen, I have a feeling we are all going to need it.' He smiled. 'And for you and your friends, Colonel Morgan, a parting gift.'

He took the key to the leg irons from his pocket and threw it to me.

I will remember that scene when Steiner spoke to the men on the waterfront till my dying day. They crowded in close because of the difficulty of hearing him above the roaring of the wind and Steiner stood on the tailboard of one of the trucks.

It had been Schellenberg's idea. At the Rectory he had obviously been very shaken by what had happened, but once we had left to drive back to the harbour in the field car he had changed, had become a different person. But then, no one was the same after that terrible day and the events which were to follow. I think it was the shrieking of the wind, the cold that seemed to touch the brain itself that drove us all a little crazy.

Schellenberg, perhaps playing himself for the first time

in his life, formulated a complete plan of action in the five minutes it took us to reach the harbour. By his reckoning there was about a hundred and twenty men he could lay his hands on without delay and time was now of vital importance. Todt workers and Pioneers in the main with a few Artillerymen thrown in, plus the rest of us. There were plenty of tools and ropes in his equipment store near the south landing stage and three heavy trucks we could use.

Getting everyone to really pull together, Germans and Todt workers alike, was something else again, which was where Steiner came in, for Schellenberg had enough sense to realise that he was the one man everyone respected.

He had to shout to make himself heard and he kept it short. 'There's a life-boat at Granville. If we can get it down here and launched into the harbour, maybe we can do something for those poor devils out there. If we can't then they drown, nothing else for it.'

As I say, I think the wind and the cold were driving men mad that day and one of the Todt workers, a small, rather insignificant man in a ragged overcoat, spoke up. He was French, from the sound of him.

'And a good thing, too. Bloody Germans. Why should we lift a finger?'

There was only the wind then and the faces, some immediately fearful at his audacity, others obviously agreeing, but too wary to say so.

'Maybe you're right,' Steiner shouted. 'I've no time to argue. If you want to help, then climb on top of the trucks. If you don't, then to hell with you. We'll still manage.'

He jumped down and for a moment, the Todt workers stayed exactly as they were, some turning to argue among themselves. Support for Steiner came from the most unexpected quarters. Fitzgerald clambered up on the tailboard and turned to face them. From the look on his face, all he needed was a sword to hold up in his right hand.

'You all know me. I'm an American and by God, when that life-boat leaves the harbour, my men will be part of its crew along with Colonel Morgan and Mr Scully who are English and Sergeant-Major Steiner and his men who are German and Austrian. Men are dying out there. Who they are doesn't matter. Now shut your mouths and get on board the trucks.'

And it worked. Not straight away, not with any sudden rush on everyone's part. I suppose thirty or forty obeyed him instantly, then a dozen followed. Perhaps with less enthusiasm, but they went. The troops had already packed into the first truck which left only a handful of Todt workers. Someone called from one of the trucks, there was a sudden chorus of voices. It was sufficient. The stragglers crowded forward and were hauled up over the tailboard of the last truck.

I was one of those in the field car which brought up the rear of the small convoy. As we moved away, another fishing boat lost its moorings and was pounded in against the breakwater, the hull splintering instantly.

I hoped it wasn't an omen.

The wind, if anything, was stronger as we went down the hill to Granville. Twigs and branches were being ripped from the beech trees in the grounds of the Seigneurie and the trucks swayed alarmingly from side to side.

One difficulty was the narrowness of the lanes. The trucks certainly couldn't get right down to the beach and unloaded on the edge of the village. But if the trucks could not negotiate those wide streets, what about the *Owen Morgan?* 11 feet 8 inches wide as I remembered. Turning the corners would be the trouble.

I raised the point with Schellenberg who nodded soberly. 'Anything which gets in the way, we knock down, but first we get the boat out.'

The boathouse had been constructed of pre-stressed concrete slabs. Schellenberg sent half-a-dozen Pioneers inside under Sergeant Schmidt, armed with ten-pound hammers and they simply smashed out the panels of the rear wall in a sustained barrage that lasted no more than two or three minutes.

The *Owen Morgan* stood exposed for all to see, trim and beautiful in her blue and white paint, showing every sign of the care Ezra had lavished on her. But she had sat there on her carriage for almost five years—five years of not being used. For the first time as I moved close, pushed by the crowd, I suddenly wondered whether she was up to it.

But there was no time for that sort of doubt now and Ezra took charge, indicating where he wanted to have the lines fixed. Fitzgerald pushed through to me, a smile on his face, 'We're moving now, eh? Have you ever known anything so splendid? Look at their faces.'

He was right. There was a new mood in the crowd, more smiles than I had ever seen there before, a kind of excitement in the air.

The ropes were thrown out, willing hands seized them. Fitzgerald grabbed for one and turned to me, his eyes shining. 'Everyone's pulling together, Morgan, don't you see that? By God, this is the most wonderful thing that ever happened to me.'

It was exactly what he needed, what his soul craved for. Humanity at its most splendidly self-sacrificing, all, as he had said himself, pulling together with real purpose. Not like war at all—nothing to do with the things he had experienced during the past few days.

On service, with crew and gear on board, the *Owen Morgan* weighed fifteen tons which was enough to haul up that narrow street. When she moved out into the rain, Ezra standing in the prow, there was a great cheer, but at once it became obvious that she would never be able to negotiate the turning at the top of the lane.

'That cottage on the corner,' shouted Ezra. 'Have it down.'

Fifty or sixty men swarmed over it with crowbars, pick-axes and hammers, crowding in so close that when the front wall caved in, several received minor injuries from the tumbling stones. Once more the heaving started and the boat was eased round into the next lane. There was a garden on that corner fronted with a five-foot wall. Schellenberg was already at work with another gang and it was flattened to the ground by the time we got there.

The main difficulty from that point was the steepness of the road up to the Seigneurie. It was awash in the heavy rain, the surface crumbling so that it was impossible for the trucks to operate at all. They moved on ahead and everyone who was able laid hands on the ropes and hauled. Men slipped, cursing wildly as they lost their footing and at one point someone screamed as the carriage slipped back, a wheel crushing his foot.

I suppose someone attended to him, but there was no time to stop. We had to keep moving. As I walked backwards, step by painful step, hauling on the rope, I could see out to Fort Victoria and the Channel beyond. It was an incredible sight. High waves with long overhanging crests and great foam patches, spray thick as mist driven headlong by the howling wind. It gave some foretaste of what lay ahead of us.

We came abreast of the Seigneurie and a crowd poured out through the gate to meet us. Medical orderlies, patients, all scrambled to find a place on one of the ropes. It was really quite amazing. Everyone wanted to be part of what was happening. For most of the people there I suppose it would be true to say they knew which way they were going for the first time in years.

Paddy Riley was there on the edge of the throng and Simone in a soldier's greatcoat. We all stopped pulling then as the trucks manoeuvred into position and the lines were hooked up quickly. I started to make my way towards Simone, but Steiner got there before me. She clutched at his arms, her face turned up to him with a look on it I had seen only once before a very long time ago, only then it had been meant for me. I turned away and the lines tightened as the trucks started to move ahead slowly.

From then on it was comparatively easy. Everyone flocked alongside, pushing and heaving on the corners, jumping for their lives when the boat rocked alarmingly on its carriage. The excitement by now was intense and rose to fever pitch when we moved past the airstrip and started down the hill towards Charlottestown.

We ran the life-boat close enough to one of the trucks for her prow to touch the tailboard and started down, everyone hanging on to the lines for dear life to stop her from running away. The truck skidded several yards at a time on the wet cobbles and the carriage with it so that the tail whipped from side to side sending men running in alarm. She scraped her paint more than once and put in two shop fronts on the way down the main street. But suddenly, we turned the last corner and there, a hundred yards below, was the harbour.

In a way, what followed was something of an anticlimax. When we reached the waterfront, we pulled her free of the truck and took her down the main access road to the lower jetty by hand. At the far end by the South Landing Stage, a stone slipway slid under the heaving waters. Steiner and the Brandenbergers joined Ezra on board, then we ran her down and into the water and tied her up.

Watching her there afloat again, grinding against the jetty, I couldn't quite take it all in. It was as if this had all happened before. In a way, I suppose it had.

Schellenberg had them roll drums of petrol down from the main store and he and Captain Warger saw to it that the tanks were filled. It was a big moment when Ezra got to work and the engines fired. I couldn't really believe it after all those years, though one had to remember that he had looked after her like a baby.

The *Owen Morgan*, as I have said, was a Watson-type motor life-boat, 41-feet long, divided into 8 water-tight compartments and filled with 145 air cases. She had twin screws driven by a couple of 35 h.p. engines and each engine was water-tight so that it could continue running even if the engine room was flooded. Her speed was 8 knots and normally, she carried a crew of eight and in rough weather, could take fifty people on board. She had two cockpits, a line-throwing gun and various other useful items of equipment.

Including Ezra, there were eleven of us in the crew. Three more than usual, but this was probably a good thing considering the lack of experience. Ezra produced R.N.L.I. yellow oilskins and life-jackets for everyone and at the moment of departure, I dare say we looked as decent a crew as the Institution could have wished to see.

I acted as second coxswain and relayed Ezra's orders. We cast off and moved away from the jetty. Steiner was acting as bowman on my suggestion and Fitzgerald was midships at the rail coiling a line. When he turned and came aft and found me in the cockpit, his eyes were shining.

He said something and smiled, but I couldn't catch his words for the wind snatched them away. Poor fool, he didn't know what he was getting into. None of them did.

14 The Wreck of the Pride of Hamburg

Men I spoke to afterwards who watched the whole affair from the shore said they had never seen anything like it which I can well believe, for when we moved past the breakwater the wind had reached hurricane force and the seas could only be described as mountainous. At a rough estimate, I would say that the height of the sea and swell must have been in the region of forty feet from crest to trough and when we went down we seemed to be going head-first to hell.

And the climb up to the next crest seemed a completely impossible task, the boat slowing almost to a halt half-way up so that for a terrifying moment, it seemed we would slide back down again. Yet each time we seemed to make it and paused for a moment before swooping onwards, screws turning madly on air.

Warger watched from the end of the breakwater and many years later he told me that the sight was something he had never been able to forget, for each time we disappeared, he never expected to see us come up again.

In these conditions it is not to be wondered that I saw fear on the faces around me. We took water constantly, great green sheets washing in from stem to stern and for a while, there was a genuine struggle for survival by some individuals.

Hagen was sluiced over the side by one great sea, but a moment or two later, was washed back on board by another. I have never seen such a look on a man's face as I saw on his when Fitzgerald and Grant dragged him into the cockpit.

Ezra had opened the side window of the wheelhouse and now he leaned out and called to me: 'See to it that every man is on a lifeline, Owen. This lot will get worse before it gets better.'

I should have thought of it earlier, although, for various reasons, lifelines are not habitually used by life-boat men. I started to work my way round, checking on everyone. Steiner was in the front cockpit with Lanz, Obermeyer and Schreiber. Lanz was being very sick, not that it mattered with the amount of water coming in and Schreiber looked terrified. Strange how relative bravery can be. It was obvious that Schreiber simply couldn't take it, should never have come. And yet in other circumstances, he had acted with what one can only term real heroism.

I shouted instructions in Steiner's ear and he nodded to show that he understood and saw to Schreiber's lifeline himself. I pulled my way back along the deck to the rear

cockpit where most of the others were and paused by the
wheel-house window to speak to Ezra. We were perhaps a
quarter of a mile out from the breakwater when disaster
struck.

It all happened so fast that it would be impossible to
say with complete certainty what went wrong. It was a
combination of things. The size of the seas breaking in,
the force of the wind striking us so hard as we teetered on
the crest of a mountainous wave that the *Owen Morgan*
sheered as it went down. The next wave struck hard on
the starboard bow and we capsized. I heard a desperate
cry, a great roaring and held on to the open window of
the wheelhouse for dear life.

The world was green water washing over me, salt in the
eyes and mouth, filling the nostrils, an unbearable weight.
We were half under and still driving on, the engines never
faltering in their watertight compartments. I started to
choke and then broke through to the surface, taking in
great lungfuls of air as we slowly righted ourselves.

I was aware of Ezra, sou'wester gone, still hanging on
to the wheel, his mouth open in a great cry, and turned to
see what had happened to the others.

Fitzgerald was safe together with Grant and Hagen, but
Wallace was missing. I turned to the rail as we topped the
next wave and caught a glimpse of yellow out there in the
green waters and then another and forced my way along
to the forward cockpit to discover that Schreiber had gone
also, his line having parted. There was nothing we could
do, I looked back, caught a last flash of yellow out there
and then we were plunging down again.

To survive in such a sea, a man needed more than a
life-jacket—he needed a miracle and it had been a long
time since I believed in those.

From then on it became more of a personal struggle for
survival than anything else. Great waves broke across us
so that both cockpits were constantly full of water. All
that we could do was hang on and leave it to Ezra and
pray.

And we were in good hands—none better, for as I have
said elsewhere, he had a genius for handling small boats
in foul weather, was one of the greatest coxswains in the
long and proud history of the life-boat service.

So terrible was the weather, so thick the veil of rain

and driven spray all around us that not once had we a
clear view of our quarry, but perhaps twenty minutes after the first capsizing, we paused for a brief moment on
top of an enormous wave and saw the Pinnacles about
three hundred yards away.

The *Pride of Hamburg* was hard on, her stern under
the water and the sea was rising and falling fifteen to
twenty feet up her hull and the waves crashed on. She had
a single tall old-fashioned funnel and straight bows and a
counter stern to go with it. The superstructure was exten-
sively damaged, half the bridge had gone and a life-boat
swung vertically in its davits which wasn't going to help
once we tried to lay alongside.

I couldn't understand why someone hadn't chopped it
free, but at that stage was not fully aware of the extent of
the tragedy which had overwhelmed her crew, did not understand the panic which seizes the mind when trapped in
such a seemingly impossible situation, faced with certain
death.

In the files of the Life-boat Institution, you may read
the official account of what happened, for Ezra submitted
his report at the first opportunity. No reason not to, for
this was one of the Institution's boats answering a call just
like any other.

Put simply, it came down to this. By varying his engine
revolutions between 600 and 700, Ezra found that he was
just able to stem the ebb tide which he thus computed was
running at about 6 knots. He had no choice, but to make
his first run in to the starboard side due to the manner in
which the *Pride of Hamburg* had gone on the reef.

The situation was about as grim as it could be and not
only because of the rise and fall of the sea up the ship's
side. There was also the starboard life-boat which someone had obviously attempted to launch and which swung
vertically from the after davit.

There were men on deck hanging on in various places
though not as many as I had expected. It was only later
that I discovered that twenty-three of her complement of
forty-eight passengers and crew were already dead including the captain, some washed overboard when she struck
and others drowned when the only life-boat to be successfully launched had been overwhelmed almost instantly by
that terrible sea.

There was a ladder in her waist down which the crew

would have to come one by one to jump, but as Ezra
made his run in and held her alongside, the life-boat
above us swung crazily and so close to the jumping ladder
that it would have been suicide for anyone to attempt to
come down.

Ezra sheered away again and lay off, using his engines
to hold us where we were. 'Got to get that bloody ship's
boat out of the way somehow,' he shouted.

Steiner was at my side, his sou'wester gone, face beaded
with water. He jumped into the cockpit and picked up an
axe. 'Take her in again, Ezra,' he cried. 'I'll try for the
ladder.'

Ezra didn't argue. There was no point for it had to be
done and without delay. The *Owen Morgan* swooped in,
turning at the last moment as he laid her alongside. A
great wave tolled in, taking her up almost to the level of
the *Pride of Hamburg's* rail and Steiner jumped for the
ladder. As the wave receded, we dropped fifteen feet with
a sickening jolt and smashed in against the hull. I was tossed into the cockpit. As I regained my feet, I saw Steiner
scrambling over the rail above.

In the same moment the suspended ship's boat sagged
and one of its oars fell to bounce across the top of the
wheelhouse into the sea. I gave one hell of a yell and as
the falls parted and the boat fell, everyone jumped for
their lives.

The ship's boat crashed on to the top of the wheelhouse, then slid over to the port side and hung across the
guard chains. Oars and various bits and pieces of equipment were scattered everywhere and Ezra was knocked to
the deck.

Another wave crashed us in against the hull of the
Pride of Hamburg and I called to Fitzgerald and Grant,
grabbed an axe and scrambled to clear the wreckage. We
fought like madmen, hacking furiously at the ship's boat,
fighting to clear her from our decks before it was too late.
It almost was. Another great sea flowed in, smashing us
against the hull and then Ezra gave the engines full power
and swung the wheel. I lost my balance again, but the
shock helped to dislodge the main portion of the wreckage. What was left of the boat slid over the port bow and
we sheered off.

I was bleeding from a cut on my forehead, Ezra was
bleeding, Grant was bleeding. Fitzgerald seemed in one

piece, yet clutched his axe as if he'd like to use it and
when he caught my eye, actually laughed out loud.

'Let's go, let's go, let's go!' he yelled. 'What are we
waiting for.'

Ezra, I now realised, had a deep gash in his forehead.
He wiped away the blood calmly and pointed through the
wheelhouse window. 'Manfred's getting them organised
from the looks of it. In we go and grab 'em as fast as you
like, Owen, You're in charge out there.'

He took her in firm up-tide to leeward and again, on
the starboard side of the *Pride of Hamburg,* allowing the
tidal current to carry us in. There were already a couple
of men on the jumping ladder well up above us, but as
another wave lifted us up, we were suddenly virtually
level. Sergeant Lanz and Fitzgerald were at the rail and
caught both men as they jumped.

One was a sailor, the other an Artillery corporal. They
crouched in the bottom of the bow cockpit and as another
wave hammered us in against the hull of the *Pride of
Hamburg,* three more started down the ladder.

I got a glimpse of Steiner leaning over the rail, waved
and then the first one jumped. Grant caught him and
pulled him down into the cockpit. The second hesitated,
then followed. He had left it too late. We dropped fifteen
feet as the wave receded and he landed heavily on top of
the wheelhouse with a cry of agony and fell from there to
the deck.

When Grant and Lanz dragged him into the cockpit he
was unconscious and obviously badly injured. The third
man hung on to the ladder with both hands, even when
we rose to his level and stayed there for a long moment so
that he could have stepped over our rail with no difficulty.
He had obviously lost his nerve.

Fitzgerald leaned over and the next time we moved up
again, grabbed him with both hands to pull him in by
force. The man screamed in panic and held on tight. A
wave pulled the life-boat twenty feet away from the hull
and Fitzgerald, refusing to let go, was dragged over the
side. He managed to grab the ladder and hung there just
below the man he was trying to save who scrambled up
the rail and climbed over.

A moment later it happened, my father all over again.
A sudden cross-current caught us hard on and pushed like
a giant hand, swinging us back against the *Pride of Ham-*

burg, trapping Fitzgerald's legs between our rail and the ladder.

He gave a great cry of agony that rose above the storm and Steiner was over the rail and grabbing for him in the moment that we started to sheer off.

The whole thing seemed to happen in slow motion. Steiner caught him with one hand and hung on to the top rung of the ladder. But it wasn't enough and as Fitzgerald started to go, I ran for the rail and jumped. I caught the bottom rung of the ladder in the trough of a wave. The next one floated me up to Fitzgerald's level and I grabbed for the ladder and got an arm around him.

Somehow we got him over the rail and when I turned, the *Owen Morgan* was sheering off again. I waved and must have decided to review the situation for with the tide ebbing fast now the whole operation could only become more difficult.

Fitzgerald was in a sorry way, both legs obviously crushed, but at least he was unconscious. There were men crouched in various places on the deck hanging on, but no one made any move to help us. We got an arm each and dragged him up the sloping deck and Steiner kicked open the first door we came to.

It was some sort of a saloon with a bar at one end and padded seats, tables bolted to the floor. A German naval officer was wedged behind one of them in a corner seat. He was in full uniform including his cap and it didn't need all the gold braid or the rows of medal ribbon to tell me that this was Korvettenkapitan Karl Olbricht. He was wearing a spinal brace, his chin held firmly in a kind of aluminum cup. It's also worth mentioning that he was clutching a bottle of rum in one hand and a glass in the other.

I kicked the door shut and the comparative quiet was uncanny. 'Come in, gentlemen,' Olbricht said in German. 'Do come in.'

He was obviously half-drunk. 'Forgive me for not standing up, but unfortunately my spine and one leg are supported by steel contraptions of one kind or another. It makes life difficult enough at the best of times. Rather more than impossible in a situation like this. What's going on out there?'

'Captain Olbricht,' Steiner said, 'Sergeant-Major Steiner, Brandenberg Division. This gentleman is Colonel Morgan, a British officer. We came in the life-boat from St Pierre to try to save you.'

Olbricht stared at me owlishly. 'British? So—we have lost the war?'

'It would take too long to explain. This is an American officer, Major Fitzgerald. He's been badly hurt. We'll have to leave him with you till we see what's happening out there.'

He was looking pretty bewildered by then though I suspect that was the drink as much as anything. When we went out on the deck I couldn't see the *Owen Morgan* at first for she was lost in the trough between two great waves. Then she soared into view unexpectedly close, but in a totally different direction.

She was circling now and turning in below the stern of the *Pride of Hamburg* which, as I have said, was under water. I suddenly realised what Ezra was going to try. A truly desperate stratagem, but one which might just work. He drove her straight in across the stern rail until his prow rested on the deck and held her in place with his engines. The men of the *Pride of Hamburg* seemed too stunned to realise what was happening. It was Steiner who galvanised them into action.

He scrambled across the sloping deck and struck out at the nearest men with clenched fists. 'Go on, damn you, get moving.'

They went at that, sliding down to the stern on their backsides. I watched five or six of them scramble over the rail into the life-boat and then the sea pulled it out again.

The tide was falling fast now and I noticed the top of the stern rail show from the water where it had been covered earlier. Ezra would not have much longer, that much was certain.

He brought the *Owen Morgan* in again, driving her up on the deck and another half-dozen were pulled to safety. That only left three waiting down there waist-deep in water as he prepared to come in again. I grabbed Steiner's arm and cried, 'Better get Fitzgerald, we haven't got long.'

We returned to the lounge. Fitzgerald was still unconscious and Olbricht looked drunker than ever. 'Time to go now, sir,' Steiner told him. 'The life-boat is down at the stern.'

'Go?' Olbricht said. 'Go where, my dear fellow? I can't even stand up. Held together with piano wire, that's me.'

'Don't argue with him,' I told Steiner. 'We'll get Fitzgerald to safety and come back for him.'

We lifted the American between us as gently as we could and went out on deck. The life-boat still waited and as we started down I saw Grant coming up the slope towards us.

Several things seemed to happen at once. A great sea rolled in and rocked the *Pride of Hamburg* so that the deck inclined even more and we lost our balance. I was close to the rail and managed to grab hold with one hand and hang on to Fitzgerald with the other.

Steiner went headlong down the slope and over the stern rail to join Grant who was already in the water. The *Owen Morgan* had been pulled out again and Ezra fought to hold her with his engines twenty yards from the stern. Both Grant and Steiner were carried alongside and lines snaked out as the crew rushed to rescue them. *The crew.* In their yellow oilskins at that distance, it was impossible to know who was German and who was American.

Again, Ezra brought the boat in, but he was already too late for it was at that period of the tide when the fall was sudden and great and the stern rail was completely clear of water. And now, he and everyone in the *Owen Morgan* were in great danger for anything might happen to them if they were swept in under the old-fashioned counter stern of the *Pride of Hamburg*.

I got my hands under Fitzgerall's armpits and started to move back up the sloping deck on my rear. It was easier than I had a right to expect or perhaps I had passed beyond that point where fatigue and physical pain are particularly noticeable. I got the door of the saloon open and pulled him inside. Olbricht was exactly where we had left him. 'Thought you were leaving,' he commented.

'So did I,' I said grimly.

I arranged cushions on the floor as a rough mattress, eased Fitzgerald on to it and went back outside. The sea seemed worse than ever, the troughs between the waves so deep that the *Owen Morgan* kept disappearing completely.

Ezra had sheered off a good fifty yards and I knew why. Now that the tide was really ebbing, jagged rocks were exposed on either side, a death trap waiting to claim anyone foolish enough to venture in.

And Ezra Scully was no fool. He had achieved a miracle. Had come out to the worst reef in the Channel Islands with a scratch crew in hurricane force winds and had saved twenty-four lives. Wiser to settle for that at the moment.

He waved from the wheelhouse, I waved back, then the *Owen Morgan* turned and started to make her slow and painful journey back to St Pierre through those mountainous seas.

15   The Mill-Race

When I went back into the saloon, Fitzgerald was moving restlessly and as I leaned over him, he moaned. I took out my knife and cut open his trousers from knee to ankle. What I discovered was anything but pleasant. He would never be able again to put one foot in front of the other from what I could see.

'He is not good, your friend?' Olbricht asked, and I realised that whatever else the drink had done, it hadn't dulled his faculties particularly. 'The captain's cabin is through there.' He nodded towards an inner door. 'End of the passage. There should be a medical kit of some description.'

The passage slanted, like the saloon, at an angle of some twenty or thirty degrees, but I didn't have too much difficulty in negotiating it. The cabin was a shambles, bedding, books, drawers, scattered everywhere. The first worthwhile find I made was a pair of binoculars in a leather case. I found a first-aid case of polished wood inside a locker above the bunk. I had only just left the cabin when the whole ship seemed to shake itself, there was an unearthly clanging, the sound of metal tearing, a thing I have heard neither before nor since. The passage then lifted abruptly to an angle of forty-five degrees.

I lost my balance and slid on my back at some speed, missing the saloon door, coming to a halt only when I hit the wall at the far end. I had the binoculars slung around my neck anyway and managed to keep a tight hold on the first-aid box, but the scramble back up the steeply inclined passage was something I achieved with difficulty.

The situation in the saloon was not without its grim humour. Olbricht still sat in the corner seat wedged firmly in place, but tilted backwards slightly. He smiled cheerfully.

'I thought we were going.'

I shook my head. 'She's settling on the reef as the sea falls back, that's all.'

Fitzgerald had rolled half under a padded bench. I pulled him back on the cushions, trying to wedge him into place and had a look in the first-aid box. I was hoping for a pain-killer and found what I was seeking in a narrow metal tray. A row of small glass ampoules of some kind of morphine derivative, each one a simple hypo.

I jabbed a couple into his left arm as directed, then got more cushions and tried to make him as comfortable as possible. He was in for a long wait because even if the wind abated, the life-boat could only get close enough to take off a man in his condition at high tide when she could float in over the rocks again. Four a.m. at the earliest and if the storm didn't blow itself out, perhaps never.

I said to Olbricht, 'I'm going on deck. I want to see if the life-boat can make it into Charlottestown. I don't know how long I'll be, but you've nothing to worry about. She won't come off the reef with the tide falling.'

'My friend, I have spent the war in submarines. I gave up worrying about anything a long time ago. If you wouldn't mind passing me a bottle of something from behind the bar, I think I might shift to exist.' He smiled wryly. 'This damned contraption I'm held together by is anything but comfortable.'

It occured to me that he was very probably in real pain. I scrambled up the sloping floor and went behind the bar. There was a great deal of broken glass about and plenty of smashed bottles, but some had survived. I took him a bottle of rum and he thanked me gravely, pulled out the cork with his teeth and drank from the bottle.

I left him and went outside. When I opened the door, the wind snatched at me with a solid, pounding force and spray cascaded across the rail. I looked over the side into a sprawing morass of jagged black rocks and white water. Beyond, the sea lifted in one enormous wave after another, all the way to St Pierre.

The binoculars were excellent. I could see the end of the breakwater, the entrance to the harbour, but not much beyond because of the driving rain and spray.

I found the *Owen Morgan* about a quarter of a mile from the *Pride of Hamburg* when she rose out of nowhere

on the crest of a wave. For a couple of seconds I had an
excellent view, could see Ezra clearly through the open
window of the wheelhouse and Steiner standing by the
bow cockpit with Grant. They disappeared again, were
out of sight for so long that with a sudden contraction of
the heart, I wondered whether they would ever come up
again.

But they did, the *Owen Morgan* rearing up out of the
sea as if by magic, disappearing again within seconds. I
stayed at the rail for the next hour, watching her progress,
staying with her every inch of that painful way. She es-
caped disaster only because she had a genius at the wheel,
I am certain of that, for the sea was the worst I have ever
seen, a sight to strike awe in the heart of any man.

The worst moment came when she was no more than a
couple of hundred yards from the breakwater. The wind
was gusting at times to as much as 100 knots and caught
the *Owen Morgan* savagely on top of a great wave. She
broached and another enormous wave carried her in sideways towards the end of the breakwater.

Remembering what had happened on another occasion,
I held my breath. Was Ezra to see another fine boat
smashed beneath him? Miraculously, her head came round
and in my mind's eye, I saw him fighting for control. At
the last moment, fate, or the lesser gods, relented. I saw
her top a final wave, then flow down into harbour and disappear behind the breakwater.

So—it was over and Ezra had made it. Ezra and his
magnificent scratch crew. Strangely enough, I felt curiously deflated. What I really needed was a drink and perhaps two. For the first time I was conscious of the cold
and of my wet clothing.

I returned to the saloon and searching again among the
bottles behind the bar, found unbelievably, a bottle of
Haig & Haig. Officers' stock, indeed. I slithered down to
Fitzgerald. He was still unconscious, but seemed quieter,
so I scrambled across to where Olbricht sat and wedged
myself behind the table next to him.

'They made it,' I said. 'I saw them enter harbour.'

'Remarkable.' He was half-way down the bottle. 'Are
they likely to be back?'

'I should think so, but they'll have to wait for the next

tide. We can expect them at any time after four in the morning.'

'I see.' He nodded. 'On the other hand, isn't it true that will be the hour of maximum danger for us? The sea can rise thirty feet or so in these waters, isn't that so? Enough with any kind of wind, to take the *Pride of Hamburg* off the rocks and in case you haven't noticed, the bottom is ripped out of her. We'll go down like a stone.'

'All right, you've managed to sum things up pretty accurately. Does it make you feel any better?'

'Not particularly, which is why I am drinking so much of this damned stuff or hadn't you noticed?'

Fitzgerald moaned, moved his head sideways and opened his eyes. I edged across to him. 'How do you feel?'

He stared at me blankly, sweat on his face, then smiled. 'Hello, Owen,' he said weakly. 'What happened?'

'You tried playing hero once too often, you daft bastard and got yourself smashed up.'

He nodded slightly. 'I remember now—my legs.' He tried to lift himself and I pushed him down. 'I can't feel anything. They don't even seem to be there.'

'Which isn't surprising,' I said. 'I've filled you full of morphine. Now be quiet and take it easy.'

He closed his eyes, then opened them again. 'So this is the *Pride of Hamburg*. What happened to the others?'

'All safely back to harbour. I watched them every inch of the way. They'll be back for you and me and Captain Olbricht here at high water in the morning.'

The drug was beginning to take effect. His eyes glazed and he said softly. 'Do you know, being out there in the *Owen Morgan* was the most wonderful thing that ever happened to me. I wouldn't have missed it for . . .'

He couldn't finish the sentence and his eyes closed.

'Dead?' Olbricht inquired.

'No, not yet.'

'He has the look, though, don't you agree?'

I did, but saying so was bad luck—the Celt in me again. I told him I was going to take a look round and went out on deck.

Water only touched the ship's hull when it was blown in by the wind for by now, a great deal more of the reef was exposed at a steep angle on a bed of jagged rocks. So far as I could see, there wasn't the slightest danger of anything nasty happening at the moment. The danger point, as Olbricht had said, was going to be when the tide started to come in again. I thought of the Mill-Race and shuddered. I had seen wrecks on the Pinnacles one day and gone the next too often for comfort.

I forced my way into what was left of the chartroom and salvaged a lantern and signalling lamp. It was late evening now, darkness moving in from the horizon and still, those mountainous seas rolled between us and the island.

I lit the lantern and hung it on a hook. Olbricht smiled. 'A little light to keep out the dark. You didn't tell me about the war, by the way. It's over, then?'

'As good as.'

He nodded gravely. 'Believe it or not, but I've been eagerly awaiting that news every day for almost six years. Now that it has finally come, it doesn't seem to mean much any more.'

Which was understandable enough. I arranged a few more seat cushions on the floor beside Fitzgerald and lay down beside him. Outside, the wind howled, rain drummed ferociously against the window. Inside, it was strangely peaceful and suddenly, I was overwhelmingly tired. I closed my eyes intending to rest them for just a little while and plunged into sleep.

I came awake to a terrible groan and found Fitzgerald struggling to sit up. I pushed him back down and when he twisted his head to look at me, his eyes were heavy with pain.

'Never known such pain. Never known such awful pain.'

'Hang on,' I said. 'I'll fix it in a minute.'

I got the other ampoule from the box and jabbed it into him. It seemed to take effect almost at once and I could see the strain ebbing from his face.

He opened his eyes and stared up into mine. 'You never liked me, did you?'

I rubbed sleep from my eyes wearily. 'Does it matter?'

'I suppose not.' He half-smiled. 'You can't win them all.'

I glanced at my watch and saw with some surprise, that it was two-thirty in the morning. 'Go back to sleep again, not long to go now.'

He didn't really hear me and spoke so softly that I had to put my ear close to his lips to hear what was said.

'Glad I came, Morgan. Heroes, all of them. Proud to have served with them. No regrets.'

Which was exactly the kind of thing I would have expected him to say. There was more, but so garbled as to not make any kind of sense. About five minutes later, he died.

Olbricht's face was grave in the lamplight. 'What now?'

I reached for the signalling lamp. 'I'm going to try to make some kind of contact with the shore and I want to see what the weather is like.'

It had stopped raining and a full moon floated in a sky of dark blue velvet studded with brilliant ice-cold stars. The wind had abated considerably, but a moderate gale was still blowing. From a rescue point of view, the whole situation had obviously changed considerably.

I could see some distance in the moonlight over the great foaming crests, but the island was shrouded in darkness. There was no sign of a light which surprised me, for it seemed likely that Ezra would have started by now and the *Owen Morgan* was equipped with an electric searchlight.

I used the signalling lamp intermittently for twenty minutes or so, but not attempting to convey any particular message. There was no need. He and the others knew we were here.

When I finally stopped, I knew in my heart that we were in trouble. The rocks were covered again now and the sea was slapping in against the *Pride of Hamburg's* hull pushing at the stern and the ship groaned uneasily.

It was about three-thirty when I scrambled back up the deck to the sheltered wheelhouse and checked the signals locker. The doors swung open and water seemed to have got to most of the boxed cartridges. I managed to find four that didn't seem too bad and a pistol to fire them and went back on deck.

The sea was over the stern at the same level it had been when Ezra had driven the *Owen Morgan* over the rail to the deck itself, only now it was still rising. The boat was moving, the stern lifting gently and already the deck was less steeply inclined. I went back to my old place at the rail and fired a signal flare. It was the kind that comes down slowly on a parachute and illuminated the entire area for a good half minute.

It was a terrifying sight out there. As the sea rose, the Mill-Race was running fast to my left, waves leaping after each other like some great river in flood. The force of it shook the boat each time it struck with a sinister, hollow clanging that reverberated throughout the hull. When the flare had drifted down into the sea, I tried the rest, but none of them were any good.

I stayed there in the darkness as a cloud obscured the moon, listening to the great rushing sound of the Mill-Race, feeling the deck vibrate under my feet and knew, with complete and utter certainty, that there would come one final moment when the *Pride of Hamburg* would be pushed from the reef and swallowed up as assuredly as if she had never existed.

I went into the saloon and Olbricht said, 'They aren't coming, are they?' I shook my head and he swallowed what was left of the rum in his bottle and sighed. 'You know, it's funny, but I never did really fancy the idea of going down with the ship.'

'I'm with you all the way there.'

'There must be something we can do. Have another look. They can't leave us here like this.'

I think I knew what was in his mind, but went anyway. The sound of the shot came as no surprise.

The ship was moving slightly from side to side now and suddenly lurged so savagely that for a terrible moment I thought that she might turn right over taking me with her.

The sea was in full spate and listening to it, I was reminded of that famous incident with Simone before the war when her dinghy had capsized and the Mill-Race had saved us. Could it do as much for me again? It didn't seem likely in a sea like that, but anything was better than staying here.

I returned to the saloon and approached Fitzgerald. It was his life-jacket I was after for two would be better than one and I could do with the extra buoyancy with those waves out there. I got it off without too much difficulty and lashed it around my own.

Olbricht had fallen forward across the table and the back of his skull was not a pleasant sight. I moved up the sloping floor and groped behind the bar among the bottles

for something worth drinking. A moment later the lantern
went out.

I went back on deck, clutching the first bottle I had laid
hand to and pulled the cork with my teeth. It was a
Schnapps and tasted as if someone had made it in the
bath. I stood at the rail and got as much of it down as I
could and watched the waters rise and the Mill-Race run.
About half was all I could take and when I tossed the bottle into the sea, my belly was on fire. At least it would
keep some of the cold out.

I had kept on all my clothes by design and now, I
picked up the signal lamp and sent a short final message
in straight morse. *Ship going now. Will have to swim for
it. Morgan.*

I could have said more, but some inner caution would
not allow it, the knowledge that Ezra and Steiner and the
others would have come by now if they had been able.
Had not come because something or someone, would not
allow it.

Radl? Always Radl. If there was trouble, it had been of
his making, of that I was certain. I pulled my eye patch
down around my neck on its elasticated band, tossed the
lamp over the rail into the sea and jumped after it.

The additional life-jacket was probably the one thing
that saved my life for the added buoyancy held me well
out of the water so that I was able to get at the air no
matter how many times waves rolled in across me.

I was sucked into the Mill-Race and carried along at a
terrific rate. In view of what followed, I would say that
the current must have been running at nine or ten knots
for the distance I covered within a few minutes was
phenomenal.

The moon was still hard and bright above and visibility
seemed much improved so that when I rose on the crest
of a wave, I could see Fort Edward on the point above
the harbour. Down I went into the valley again, caught in
the current that bore me along as helplessly as a wooden
spar.

It wasn't particularly cold at first—the clothing helped
there. The cold came later, but I tried to make as little
movement as possible to conserve body heat.

There was no real sense of passing time. My watch was
waterproof and luminous, I checked it and discovered

with a shock that I had been in the water twenty minutes
at least. In the east, the edge of night was touched with
light. Another great sea lifted me high and I caught a last
glimpse of the *Pride of Hamburg* still fast on the Pinnacles. And then, beyond her, a wall of white water rolled in
from the Atlantic carrying all before it. It washed the reef
in an enormous curtain of spray and when it cleared, the
Pride of Hamburg had disappeared for ever.

Time really did cease to exist then as I let the current
take me where it wanted. On another occasion it had carried us in to Steiner's beach, but would it now?

Steiner's beach? Strange how it had become that so that
I could never think of it in any other way. Time is so
relative after all and so very much can be squeezed into
one brief period, more perhaps than in the rest of a lifetime.

I was cold now and my face and eyes were sore from
the salt. Visibility was not quite so good, the moon was
down, dawn coming up and the cliffs were dark shadows,
Fort Marie Louise standing stark above them like something from another time, another place.

If I missed, if I was on the outer edge of the current, I
would be carried past the south-east corner of the island
and Brittany was a hell of a sight farther on. I'd reach
there all right, but at some future date and fit only for fish
bait.

I was tired—completely at the end of my tether. My
head lolled forward and then, lifted high on a wave, I
looked across the ragged white carpet of surf to the cliffs
black in the gray dawning and saw beneath them, the
beach—Steiner's beach. A voice called my name, high and
clear, like a distant trumpet echoing from the past, from
childhood. Was it then or now? I went under, struggled to
the surface again and another wave lifted me high so that
I saw her sharp and clear, thigh-deep in water, hair blowing in the wind. Simone waiting for me—waiting for the
Mill-Race to bring me in as it had brought us in together
so long ago.

The waters rolled in, relentless, implacable, a great
stinking wave tossed me to the moon and back, filling my
throat with the hard taste of the salt and the current took
me in, lifting me in its hard hand, taking me in to the
beach in a final rush.

The sea was in my ears, inside my head, my hands clawed at a waterfall of gravel. The sea came in again, flailing my body trying to draw me back. I screamed, certainty deserting me for the first time since leaving the *Pride of Hamburg*. I clawed frantically at air and found a hand—a hand that gripped mine with the strength of iron fused on iron.

I was on my back and someone seemed to be hitting me with a hammer between the shoulder blades. I kept on coughing and then vomited a great quantity of water.

After a while, I managed to croak, 'All right—enough. I'll live.'

I turned and Simone, who was on her knees beside me, flung her arms round my neck. 'Thank God, Owen. I knew you would try the Mill-Race. Paddy and Ezra wouldn't believe it possible, but I knew you would try.'

They were crouched on the other side of me and Ezra passed a flask across. 'Drink some of that. What happened to Major Fitzgerald?' I told him between pulls at his flask and he nodded sadly. 'I thought as much when I saw your signal, but they wouldn't let me reply.'

I stared at him blankly and Paddy said, 'Radl killed Major Brandt at the rectory late yesterday afternoon. We don't know how. He was waiting at the jetty with his S.S. when the life-boat came in.'

'Which was why we couldn't come back for you, lad,' Ezra explained.

I struggled up. 'And Steiner?'

'Radl's going to hang him from the old beech tree by the church gate for the whole world to see. Troops and Todt workers alike. Make an example of him, see?'

'When?' I demanded slowly and the voice seemed to belong to someone else.

'It's fixed for eight o'clock.' Riley glanced at his watch. 'Which gives him about an hour and I wouldn't allow much for your American friends' chances afterwards.'

Simone started to sob bitterly.

No bodies floated in to the beach below as I scrambled down the face of the cliff above Horseshoe, but otherwise things were exactly as they had been on that first morning. It was raining steadily and Fort Victoria was barely visible in the dawn mist.

I found my reefer coat at the back of the crevasse where I had left it and the Mauser with the S.S. bulbous silencer in the pocket. I still wore my yellow oilskin from the life-boat. I discarded it now, shivering in the cold air and pulled on the reefer coat and the old bosun's cap I had stuffed into the pocket.

So, now I was ready, the same man who had landed by night, had crouched here on this ledge a century ago. The same and yet not the same. I sniffed the cold air with a conscious pleasure and the same thought went through my mind as it had done before. *A good morning—a fine morning to die in.* If that was to be the end, then let it be so.

I scrambled back up the cliff to where Paddy Riley's old car was parked, his one concession from the Germans as the only medical man on the island. He was inside with Simone, but Ezra stood in the rain filling his old pipe with some of that terrible home-grown French tobacco he favoured.

'Found what you wanted then?' he commented. 'Your Dad's old coat, isn't it?'

'That's right, Ezra.'

'Round the Horn and back twice in that under sail and me with him.'

I took the Mauser from my pocket, pulled the clip from the butt and emptied it. There were seven rounds left. I reloaded it carefully, then rammed the clip back into the butt.

'Not thinking of taking on the whole bloody world with that are you?' he said.

'If necessary. I'm not leaving Steiner to hang if that's what you mean and those Rangers, in case you've forgotten, are under my command.'

'Be sensible, lad. Radl's a first-class swine, but he knows what he's doing. He's got twenty-two S.S. paratroopers down there—men from his old regiment. They'd hang, draw and quarter you if he gave the word. If he ordered them to jump off the top of Fort Edward two hundred foot into the sea, they'd do it.'

'Suicide for you to go down into Charlottestown now, Owen,' Paddy Riley put in. 'Radl thinks you're dead which at least gives you a chance to keep on living.'

'An interesting observation,' I said. 'Reminds me of a story I once heard about a respectable, forty-five year old Dublin physician who spent his spare time back in 1920 as medical officer to an I.R.A. flying column in Connemara. He didn't seem to find the idea of a few thousand guerrillas taking on the entire British Army at all unreasonable.'

His bony nose twitched and he raised a hand defensively. 'All right, I surrender, but only if I can play, too. I might as well go out with a bang.' He opened the Gladstone bag at his feet and produced an old-fashioned British service revolver. 'I've had this around for a hell of a long while, Owen. Time I put it to use again.'

'You must be mad, both of you,' Ezra said. 'The odds are impossible.'

'You're quite right.' I nodded. 'Just like taking a lifeboat out to the most dangerous reef on the North Atlantic seaboard with a scratch crew in hurricane conditions.'

He swallowed hard on that one and Simone came in then, tense and very, very pale. 'You'll try, Owen, you'll get him out?'

'I'm an expert at taking on the world on my own in spite of what Ezra thinks,' I said, 'I've had five years practice at this kind of game. Now let's get down to Charlottestown and see what's happening.'

Which all had a nice, confident ring to it. For a while there, I almost had myself believing it.

Just past the airstrip on the other side of the road, there was the main water tower standing on the crest of the hill above Charlottestown. From there, the view was panoramic, every street, every back alley, all the way down to the harbour, just like a model.

The church bell was tolling, a nice, macabre touch that. Obviously Radl was enjoying himself. Riley had a pair of excellent Zeiss glasses in the car and he got them out and focused them on the churchyard.

When he passed them across, his face was grave. 'It doesn't look good, Owen.'

The church and the cemetery jumped into view. The whole thing had obviously been organised for maximum effect. There were at least a hundred and fifty Todt workers in several long lines against the wall. In front of them, forty or fifty Pioneers were drawn up, all with rifles. Sergeant Schmidt was out in front wearing a side arm.

Which made me wonder about Schellenberg. I soon found him. He was standing beside Grant and Hagen, the two surviving Rangers and there was an S.S. man to each of them holding a machine pistol, which didn't look too good for Schellenberg.

I searched for the Brandenbergers and found Lanz, Obermeyer and Hilldorf standing at the main gate guarded by three military policemen whose brass breastplates glinted dully in the gray light.

There was no sign of Steiner, but everyone was obviously waiting for something, presumably Radl's arrival and the great double iron gates already stood wide. The interesting thing was that the old Westminster Bank building that housed the Platzkommandantur, backed on to the cemetery. The first floor windows of the house next to it, the signals headquarters, were open and provided a grandstand view. Through the field-glasses I could see a couple of soldiers watching, but standing well back in the room, probably wary of Radl's wrath.

It was like the old days again working undercover in France. There was never enough time then either. You had to learn to assess the situation in a matter of minutes, find your soft spot and move in fast. When I lowered the glasses, Simone took them from me.

'The signals headquarters next to the Platzkommandantur,' I said. 'What's it like inside?'

'The old Grouville house,' Paddy told me. 'You must have been in a hundred times.'

'But what is it like now?' I demanded.

'I've been in a time or two,' Ezra said. 'Downstairs is sleeping quarters. Radio room in what used to be the drawing room on the first floor at the back of the house overlooking the churchyard.'

'How many men?'

'Sometimes only the duty operator, but I've known three or four to be in there on occasion. Why?'

'It looks like the weak spot to me. I might be able to get a shot at Radl from there.'

'And what good would that do?'

'The war is as good as over and most of the troops down there know it.' I shrugged. 'With Radl gone, they might take a completely different view of the whole situation. They all respect Steiner, remember.'

'Including the S.S. boys? How do they react if anything happens to Radl?'

Simone gave a sudden gasp and I took the glasses from her and focused them. Steiner was being marched in through the gates between two S.S. men. They came to a halt beneath the beech tree.

It was exactly ten minutes to eight. 'The scene is set,' I said. 'All it needs now is Radl. Are you two with me?'

It was Ezra I was really speaking to and he knew it. He sighed and nodded. 'Aye, I'll do anything you want, Owen. When it comes right down to it, I'll not stand by and see that lad hang without raising a finger.'

'Right, then get me down to that signals headquarters as fast as you like and I'll explain what we do on the way.'

I got on the floor in the rear and Simone covered me with an old blanket. We didn't have much time, but what there was, we could count on. I was sure of that. If Radl had set the execution for eight a.m. then eight a.m. he meant, nothing was more certain.

When we braked to a halt, Ezra got out first and then Simone. There was a pause and then Riley whispered, 'Quick as you like, Owen.'

I went out crouching and found Ezra in the porch of what had always been the old Grouville house to me, holding the door open. I went through into the hall, the Mauser ready against my thigh.

It was dark and gloomy and signs of military occupation were everywhere. The carpets had gone and the whole place could have done with a couple of coats of fresh paint. Even the beautiful old Wedgewood plaques on the wall had been chipped and defaced.

There was still the gold framed cheval mirror on the wall at the end and a small, dark man waited for me there in the shadows, strangely menacing. But he had been with me for some time now, this man who could kill so readily and efficiently.

I went up the stairs cautiously, Riley and Ezra behind, telling Simone to stay in the hall. Riley had the old .45 ready in his hand and I whispered, 'Don't use that unless you really have to. I'd rather do this quietly.'

I opened the door gently and stepped into the room. There was bank of radio equipment to one side, an operator on duty in headphones. A signals sergeant stood peering out of the window, an S.S. man with him, a Schmeisser sub-machine gun slung from his shoulder.

The wireless operator saw me first, his eyes widened and I put a finger to my lips and brought up the Mauser. I tiptoed forward and touched its cold muzzle to the back of the S.S. man's neck. He stiffened and I reached over and eased the Schmeisser from his shoulder.

I gave it to Ezra and stepped back. 'Turn round both of you and move away from the window. This thing is silenced, in case you didn't know, so behave.'

They did exactly as they were told, but the reactions were different. The signals sergeant simply looked wary whereas the S.S. man eyed me calculatingly, not in the least put out, obviously looking for his moment to move.

'Against the wall,' I said and outside there was the sound of a car.

Riley glanced out of the window. 'Radl's just arriving.'

The Mercedes had halted just inside the gate and Radl was standing up in the back seat. He was in his best uniform and looked very impressive.

'Can you get him from here?' Riley demanded.

'I should imagine so. I've done it before in worse conditions than this.'

It was no more than a couple of minutes to eight and the wireless operator jumped up and said in a low, urgent voice, 'Please, Colonel Morgan, don't kill us. It would be foolish. The war is almost over. They have arranged a meeting to discuss terms at Luneberg.'

'Shut your mouth,' the S.S. man ordered.

'But it is true.' The wireless operator turned to me desperately. 'I've just heard the news bulletin put out by the B.B.C.'

And there was my answer. So simple. So beautifully simple. I turned to the signals sergeant. 'Lean out of that window right now and tell them that the war is over. That it's just come in over the radio from Guernsey. Top of your voice so everyone can hear.'

There was an expression of genuine shock on his face. 'But I couldn't do that. Colonel Radl would have me shot.'

The S.S. man obliged me by choosing that precise moment to jump for another Schmeisser hanging from a peg behind the door. I shot him in the back of the head and he fell across a table and rolled to the floor, killed instantly.

I extended my arm and touched the signals sergeant between the eyes with the bulbous end of the Mauser. 'Three seconds, that's all you have. If Steiner dies, you die.'

The room was filled with the stench of cordite and blood had sprayed across the far wall by the door. There was a pause that seemed endless, one of those eternal moments in time that one never forgets and then the sergeant turned, sick and frightened and stumbled to the window.

They had the rope around Steiner's neck and were about to throw the other end over the branch twenty feet above. As I moved in behind the signals sergeant, peering over his shoulder, a diversion came from a completely unexpected source.

Simone appeared in the main gateway. She stood there peering in, saw Steiner and what was happening and gave a terrible cry. It definitely spoiled Radl's beautiful show. Everyone turned and there was a sudden hubbub as she ran past the Mercedes.

She had almost got to Steiner when one of the S.S. guards reached her. She gave him a hard time, kicking and struggling wildly. What happened then didn't help Radl one little bit. The S.S. man, losing patience, struck her in the face with his clenched fist, knocking her to the ground.

There was not a man there, German or otherwise, who had not received some kindness from her if only in words. She had worked in the hospital, nursed them in sickness, but more than that—she was the only woman on the island. The only woman most of them had seen in a year or more which put her in a very special light indeed.

There was a sudden angry roar. Not only the Todt workers surged forward, but the Pioneers and Artillerymen too, some of them holding their rifles in a very business-like way.

Radl shouted, trying to make himself heard and I knew that it was now or never. 'Give me that damned cannon of yours,' I said to Riley and grabbed it from his hand.

I'd forgotten just how loud these old Webleys could sound. I fired twice out of the window and the reports thundered across the churchyard, mingling with the tolling of the bell and produced instantaneous silence. Every face turned in astonishment and I rammed the barrel of the .45 into the back of the signals sergeant's skull, keeping well behind him.

'Now!' I told him savagely. 'Start shouting or I'll blow your head off.'

He did me proud. 'The war!' he screamed. 'The war is over! We've just received the news from Guernsey on the radio!'

The silence continued for what seemed like an eternity, but an eternity which in reality lasted for no longer than twenty seconds and then the crowd seemed to erupt into sound and action. The roar could have been heard at the other end of the island and must have caused considerable alarm to those men on duty at various coastal defences.

Everyone seemed to move at once, the Todt workers, the Pioneers, all flooding across the churchyard through the gravestones to where Steiner stood beneath the tree. They swarmed around him, the rope came down.

I could see the helmets of the S.S. guards here and there as they fought their way back towards Radl in the Mercedes at the gate. There was no shooting—no violence that I could see. They had wanted to save Steiner, all of them, and for the moment, that was their sole aim.

I don't know what happened then. Perhaps one of the S.S. men panicked. There was a sudden stutter of a machine pistol, the crowd scattered leaving three of their number on the ground.

One of them was a German, a Pioneer and the effect on his comrades was astonishing. Several of them raised their rifles and fired and two of the S.S. men round Radl's car fell.

And then I saw Steiner. He ran through the crowd waving his arms and calling to them. The Pioneers lowered their rifles, there was a sudden stillness as he moved out into no man's land between the two sides.

I could hear him clearly in the silence which followed,

for by now, even the church bell had stopped tolling. He stood, hands on hips, in direct confrontation with Radl in the back of the Mercedes, then turned to the crowd.

'No shooting, no more killing, It is all over, don't you understand? We've survived the bloody war, all of us.'

Radl pulled out his Luger and shot him twice in the back.

Everything happened at once after that. I leaned out of the window to get a shot at him and found the Mercedes already reversing through the gate, the S.S. paratroopers going back with it, firing steadily.

Most of the people in the crowd had the good sense to go down after Steiner's shooting and it didn't look to me as if a great deal of damage had been done. I went out of the radio room on the run and took the stairs three at a time!

The door to the street stood open and as I reached the hall, the Mercedes lurched by, at least a dozen S.S. hanging on. Another five or six ran after it. I let them get past the door, then moved out, dropped to the cobbles and started firing.

I wasn't alone. Riley was on the ground beside me, the blast of his old .45 like the cannon at Waterloo and Ezra stood by the porch firing a Schmeisser. Confined in that narrow street the S.S. who were on foot didn't stand a chance. As the Mercedes accelerated round the corner at the bottom, they turned, firing desperately and went down within seconds.

When I glanced back over my shoulder I found that we had not been fighting alone. Schellenberg was there, a rifle in his hands, at least a dozen Pioneers at his back together with three of Brandt's military police and the Brandenbergers, all carrying rifles.

Paddy Riley was already running past them towards the churchyard, and I went after him. There was a hell of a crowd in there, everyone shouting excitedly and I saw Grant and Hagen swinging rifles savagely, beating them back, clearing a space for Riley.

Steiner lay on his back, eyes fixed on some point, high in the sky. There was blood on his face, mingling with the rain, soaking into the front of his tunic where one of the bullets had exited. Simone knelt beside him. She looked

dazed and shocked, obviously still suffering from the effect
of that savage blow in the face. I don't think she realised
just how bad he was.

Grant and Hagen stared at me incredulously as I
pushed past them and dropped to one knee beside Riley.
'It's bad, Owen. I won't pretend otherwise.'

'Owen?' Steiner's eyes flickered. 'Owen, is that you?'

I leaned over and patted him clumsily. 'As ever was,
Manfred. Came floating in on the tide with the rest of the
flotsam.'

'I always said you had qualities.' His hand went to his
throat, felt for the Knight's Cross and tore it free in one
convulsive movement. He held it out to me blindly. 'For
you, Owen, you've earned it. Look after Simone. Always
that, promise me.'

I searched for words but I was too late. His eyes closed,
his head went to one side. Simone gave a cry like an animal in pain and fainted across him.

If I die, see that he does, can I ask that much of you?
The words echoed in my ears from that day on the
beach at Granville and my own reply. I stared blindly at
the Knight's Cross in my right hand, then put it away
carefully in my pocket and pushed through the crowd
towards the gate where Schellenberg and his men waited.
A hand caught at my shoulder and spun me round. I
looked up into Grant's tortured face.

'What happened to the Major?'

'He died on the *Pride of Hamburg* before it went
down,' I told him. 'He was badly injured. He needed a
doctor and there wasn't one there, it was as simple as that.
I did what I could for him. I'm sorry.'

The pain in that great iron face was terrible to see. 'We
could have gone back. We could have gone back for him,
but Radl wouldn't let us.' He was shaking in a kind of
uncontrollable rage. 'By God, I'll have that bastard for
this.'

I moved on to the gate. They were all there by then.
What was left of the Brandenbergers, Schellenberg and his
Pioneers, Sergeant Schmidt who had seen his best friend
hung like a dog, Brandt's policemen—all of them men
with some account to settle with Radl.

There was the clatter of boots on the cobbles and a Pioneer corporal pushed through the crowd and saluted

Schellenberg. 'I cut through Fish Street and climbed the new water tower,' he said. 'They've taken the road to Fort Edward.'

Schellenberg turned to me, blood on his forehead, his steel spectacles slightly askew. He straightened them, then stood to attention. 'Colonel Morgan, I now consider myself and my men to be under your command. What are your orders?'

There was a sudden silence while everyone waited. Grant turned slowly and looked at me, a kind of agonised appeal on his face and I nodded. 'Right, let's go and get the bastard.'

17   An End to Killing

The hunt was up now with a vengeance. At the top of the main street was the old island transport company's yard which the Germans had used as a vehicle maintenance depot. We found everything we needed in the way of arms in the ammunition store there and commandeered a three-ton truck and a half-track troop carrier with a heavy machine gun mounted in the back.

My plan, if plan you could call it, was to get after him fast and hit him hard before he could establish his defences. He had no more than twelve or fifteen of his S.S. left now, but they were first-class fighting men, veterans every one and rooting them out of the fort could prove a costly business.

According to Schellenberg, there were no more than a dozen Artillerymen on duty up there at the present time, which could have been worse, even if they did choose to obey Radl's orders which was not only likely, but understandable.

We braked to a halt just below the crest of the hill where the road lifted to the fort and I had a quick look at the situation through the field glasses Schellenberg had provided. The main gates were closed and a couple of S.S. helmets showed above the sandbags of the machine gun post outside. I thought about it for at least ten seconds, then made my decision.

'The troop carrier goes in first. The only way we'll get

through those gates. I want three men. One at the wheel
and two on the machine gun. Everyone else into the
truck.'

Sergeant Schmidt, who had been driving the troop carrier anyway, peered out through the open visor at me. 'I
might as well stay where I am. I know what I'm doing
with these things.'

Lanz and Obermeyer had already taken their stations at
the machine gun, so there was really nothing to argue
about. I got into the cab of the truck beside Schellenberg
and we followed the troop carrier, allowing a twenty yard
interval. The half tracks threw mud and filth in a great
cloud from the broken surface of the road as Schmidt
turned on the speed.

The machine gun beside the gate started to fire when
we still had a hundred yards to go, but the troop carrier
took the brunt, the bullets glancing harmlessly from its ar-
moured plating.

Lanz and Obermeyer were replying in kind, but without
a great deal of effect, their fire shredding the sandbags
and raising such a cloud of dust that it was difficult to see
what was happening up there.

The troop carrier hit the gates at something approaching fifty miles an hour, tearing them from their
hinges. The vehicle shuddered, losing half its speed so that
the distance between us was halved and as we passed the
machine gun post, Schellenberg who had been nursing a
stick grenade, leaned out of the open window and
dropped it into the two pale faces dimly seen through the
dust cloud. The explosion rocked the truck as we roared
under the granite archway with Victoria Regina and the
date 1856 carved above it and bounced across the broken
gates.

The troop carrier swung broadside on. I saw Obermeyer
go over the side clutching a bloody face, Lanz swing,
working the machine gun. There were men up on the
rampart above the courtyard, S.S. by their helmets, firing
furiously. A couple bounced down into the yard and the
troop carrier slewed and smashed into a truck that was
parked by the steps on the other side.

The truck braked to a halt and we all got out fast. I
saw Hilldorf run forward and get the side door of the
troop carrier open. Lanz had already dragged Schmidt
from behind the wheel. He rolled him down to Hilldorf

and jumped after him. They got an arm each and started to run for the shelter of the archway by the steps and reached it with half-a-second to spare. The petrol tank of the troop carrier exploded like a bomb, showering burning fuel over a wide area. The truck it had collided with, started to burn furiously and within seconds, a dense pall of black smoke had drifted across the courtyard.

From then on it was a kind of nightmare, every man for himself, continuous action in which one never stopped running. I picked up a Schmeisser someone had dropped and went up the steps to the south rampart. I saw figures dimly through the smoke, fired, and kept on firing. Grant was at my shoulder, Hagen just behind him.

I tripped over a body and almost lost my balance. As the clip emptied, a figure loomed out of the smoke, an S.S. sergeant, eyes rolling, teeth bared in a kind of rictus. I threw the Schmeisser into his face. He ducked and came up shouting, his machine pistol levelled on my middle. Grant and Hagen fired at the same moment driving him back into the smoke.

There was firing all around me, the deafening explosion of a grenade, voices calling savagely, a sudden scream. I stumbled over the top step and found myself on another level, smoke eddying in the wind. I held the Mauser in my hand now, a figure emerged from the gloom firing. Hagen cried out and went down and in his place was Schellenberg. The smoke cleared even more and there were three of them perhaps ten yards from us. Schellenberg dropped to one knee holding his Luger in both hands as to the manner born, firing coolly. He gave a sudden cry, clapped a hand to his face and sagged to one side.

There was only one figure there now still coming on. I emptied the Mauser into him, saw him sway and fall and then a great gust of wind blew in from the sea dissolving the smoke like magic.

I was on the final high point of the fort and Radl stood there no more than five yards away, a machine pistol in his hands. He did not recognize me then, had no chance, for suddenly, Grant was between us, his hands reaching out to destroy. Radl emptied the Schmeisser into him and still Grant kept on going. He almost made it, but not quite and fell on his face no more than a couple of feet away from the man he had died hating.

I went in on the run, but already I was too late. Radl's

hand came up holding a Luger, and then a strange thing happened. He recognized me—saw the dead walk before him and the shock of it was like a physical blow.

He hesitated, his finger slackening on the trigger, my name a whisper on his lips. The gutting knife was ready in my hand. As I swung, the blade jumped, catching him under the chin, shearing up through the roof of his mouth into the brain. He fired the Luger convulsively into the ground, dropped it and clutched at me. It took all the strength I possessed to pull that knife free. He swayed there for a moment, glaring at me, then fell backwards across the low parapet, down to the sea breaking in across those black rocks below.

I stayed there for a long, long moment, then cleaned the knife mechanically on my coat, closed it and put it in my pocket. As I turned, Schellenberg emerged from the smoke clutching a bloody handkerchief to his face. He only managed to speak with an effort, but what he did say summed it all up admirably.

'It still doesn't make up for Steiner.'

But there was nothing I could say to that and I moved past him and went down through the smoke and carnage to the courtyard.

I found a field car down there, climbed behind the wheel and drove back to Charlottestown. I was tired—more tired than I had been in my life before. Too much had happened in too short a time. Too much destruction. Too much killing.

The main street was crowded with Todt workers and German troops wandering about aimlessly. For them, too, something had finished and they were trapped in that limbo that always exists between old ends and new beginnings.

I drove up past the church slowly and saw Ezra come out of the churchyard. He waved and ran towards me. 'What happened up there?'

I told him, but strangely enough, he didn't seem all that interested. 'I'm looking for Simone. She's disappeared. She came up to the hospital with us when we took Manfred, but she couldn't stand the waiting.'

I stared at him, unable to take it in properly. 'Are you telling me that Steiner is alive.'

'He's in a bad way all right, but it wasn't as final as it looked when Paddy got him on the slab. One bullet had gone straight though a lung, the other turned on his ribs. He'll live.'

'And Simone doesn't know this?'

He nodded. 'God knows where she is now, poor child.'

But I did, with something like certainty.

I could see her at the edge of the water from the top of the cliffs and I started down the path past the notice that warned of mines. Frankly, I don't know how I made it because all of a sudden my limbs felt like rubber and once or twice I stumbled and almost lost my balance.

I dropped into the soft sand at the bottom of the path, rested for a minute or so then got up and went towards her. She turned to meet me, her eyes swollen with weeping and my heart went out to her.

She came into my arms as she had done so many times before and I smoothed her hair. 'He's going to be all right, Simone. That's the big thing he and I have in common. We're both survivors.'

Her head came up slowly, eyes burning. 'Manfred is alive? Are you telling me that Manfred is alive?'

She pulled away and ran across the beach, stumbling in the loose sand, sobbing hysterically. I watched her scramble over the rocks to the bottom of the path and start to climb.

It didn't feel anything like as bad as I had thought it would to see her go. I suppose, in my heart, I'd already got used to the idea. It was very pleasant there with the sea rolling in over the soft white sand and for no earthly reason that I could account for, I thought of Mary Barton and wanted her near me with an intensity that was something of a revelation.

I slumped down into the sand. I was smiling, because in a strange way, life began again. It was all over. Not just the events of the previous week or so, but everything that had gone to make up the last six years. And what did I have to show for it? One eye and the Knight's Cross. Henry would appreciate that. Life was funny, whichever way you looked at it.

There was really only one thing left that I hadn't attended to. My hand went into my pocket and came out holding the gutting knife. I sprang the blade and threw it out to sea with all my strength. It glinted once, then disappeared into those grey waters for ever.

A storm petrel cried harshly as it dipped above my head and flew away. I got to my feet; walked back across the sands and slowly, very slowly, started to climb the path.